HOTEL OBLIVION

Underground Voices

http://www.undergroundvoices.com

Edited by Cetywa Powell

ISBN: 978-0-9830456-2-5

Printed in the United States of America.

GUEST LIST & ROOM NUMBERS

Room 5
ANDREW CUSICK

Shotgun

The man sat inside the Lancer, his shape cloaked in browns and greens, his skin split and raw. A white dress draped over the body of his wife, her figure sun-kissed and tired, her stature reposed in evening shadow. In the center of her nape lay the pale, tanless mark of where a necklace had been pawned off the week before. The radio told a common story: race gangs brutally murdering blacks at random, and the woman reached over to silence the ugly interruption.

He asked for the Lupara in the back and the woman reached around and handed it to him dutifully, carefully enough to not wake the child strapped in the middle seat. The car's interior was cluttered with boxes and bags and other assorted items, the family's path pigeonholed to vagrancy. The child was theirs. Its name was undecided still despite the seven months it had been breathing.

The man removed a cigarette from his front right pocket. He sucked on it anxiously and his wife shook her head though neither of them had spoken.

The sky was steeped in setting sun and the clouds were purple with dusk. All around them lay endless fields of corn and wheatgrass, dried up in the brutal drought that had hit the West in recent weeks. The highway, though physically empty, remained populated, brimming with the ghostly carriages of restless vagabonds long since released from heartbeats of ceaseless travel and frequent death—failed vagrants whose journey to the California coastline remained incomplete. A tumbleweed moved across the asphalt in the grips of an elemental ballet. The silence was broken.

"You're going to die," she said, shaking her head.

"No, I'm not," the man replied, his face unmoved.

She turned around and looked at their son. "One of these days."

"You think too much."

"Well, you don't think at all, dammit," she said. The woman pulled out a wrinkled juice-box from her pocket and punched a hole in it for the straw.

The man twisted the handle and the passenger door opened. "I'll be back in an hour. We'll leave tomorrow morning."

"For where?" she said quickly.

He paused, but did not turn to face her. "Home."

"Do you mean that?" she said, hope flickering in her voice.

"Yes."

They faced each other.

"I'll be back in an hour," he repeated.

She smiled faintly.

"I love you," she said.

"I know," he responded, unmoved.

The man turned to face his wife and the baby began to cry.

"The hose is leaking, but you should be able to make it back to the motel," he said.

"Yeah," she coughed, "I hope."

The man put the small shotgun inside his shirt, burying it in the makeshift pouch he'd cut out of the inside a few days before. He opened the door and stepped out of the car and his wife turned to tend to the child. The man shut the door behind him and unhooked the pump from the gasket, and a thin stream of gasoline dripped down his fingers as the lifeblood of his family revved itself into function.

As the car pulled away the boy opened his eyes and looked at his father, who smiled and held his hand up to say goodbye, even though the child was too young to understand.

The car moved off the gravel lot and onto the highway, revving off into the setting sun, leaving a whirlwind of dust in its wake.

The man was alone.

An American flag flew outside the station, the banner's center marked with a strange, flapping puncture. A vulture sat perched at the tear, picking away at the remains of some of the stars that had been ripped out. About a hundred feet below rested a tortoise, its shell half-splintered. It took refuge in the shade amongst a candy wrapper, a dried piece of bubble gum, and a patch of weeds scorched by Nevada summer, its body barely visible next to the glass door that served as the station's entrance. The gas station itself was entirely bare, save for a single car in the lot, the owners', a '57 Beetle, azure and beaten down by age.

He slowly stepped past the Beetle, opened the door, and went inside. Air rushed over him, its processed smell taking his nostrils and its cool, recycled chill grazing his cracked summer skin. Behind the counter stood another, a wiry, thin, grey-haired black man. He wore a stained white T-shirt and a pair of jeans, a speck of dribble glued to the side of his mouth.

The man pulled out a wad of cash from his pocket and paid for the services without a word, holding onto his chest to be sure the shotgun remained invisible.

"Five twenty five. Exact change," he said.

The clerk said nothing as he rang up his customer, and the man considered drawing the shotgun at that point, but he stopped himself when he saw a shadow move behind the counter, an unseen figure. As the clerk handed back the receipt he spoke.

"The name's Marcus," he said, holding out his hand.

"It's nice to meet you," the man said, outstretching his hand.

"I saw your woman left without you," Marcus said.

"That's right," the man replied quietly.

"Well then there's another car here that you're hiding?"

The man put his wallet into his back pocket. "Not that I'm aware of."

"Then she's coming back?" he responded quickly.

"I would hope so."

Marcus looked up sharply. "When?"

"A few minutes," the man said.

For a moment they both hesitated.

"A few minutes?"

"Yeah, that's what I said," the man responded. He paused accidentally. "She's dropping the boy off at her mother's place."

"Where's that?" Marcus asked.

The man's expression stayed flat.

"Edenia Lane, a few miles north of 376."

A woman stepped out from behind the counter, the shadow from before. She was grey, much greyer than the man. She was weathered and beautiful. She stared at the clerk for a moment.

"Marcus," she said calmly, "don't be so nosy."

"I'm not being nosy, Denise, I'm being cautious," Marcus

responded, his eyes locked on the other man.

"Did you see the tortoise on your way in?" she prompted.

"What?" The man said.

"The turtle outside. Did you see it?"

"No, I guess I missed it ma'am," the man said.

"He's lived here for seven months."

"Yours?"

"I suppose. He's been around since our daughter left."

"Good to hear," the man nodded nervously, his teeth digging deep into his lower lip.

A moment passed between the three before Marcus cut it off.

"You're from around here then?" Marcus said.

"No. My home isn't around here, mister," the man responded.

"Whereabouts then?"

"The San Fernando Valley," the man spoke, slowly and deliberately.

"We've lived here for forty years. We raised a family here," Marcus said.

He paused and chuckled to himself faintly. "You raised a black family around here?"

"Yes."

The other man nodded and gazed outside thoughtfully. "Bold move."

"The right move."

Denise stepped forward now. She was smaller than Marcus, much smaller, and she took her husband's hand and rubbed it gently, her eyes fixed on their newest customer.

"I made some sandwiches," she said. "Meat and cheese. If you were hungry you could have one."

The man stared at her, his hands firm on the shotgun beneath his shirt.

"That's not necessary," he said.

The woman gestured towards her husband. "Marcus, why don't you go into the back and grab some sandwiches?"

"The man said he wasn't hungry."

"I'm asking you, Marcus," she added firmly.

"It doesn't sound like asking to me."

"Well then, I'm telling you politely."

"Polite in your eyes," Marcus said, stepping away slowly. He passed through a door behind the counter but turned to face the man as he left. Denise kept her eyes fixed.

When her husband was out of earshot she spoke: "California."

"I'm sorry?" the man asked.

"You said you were from California."

"That's right. Born and raised."

"I always liked the people I meet from California. They always seem like they're getting somewhere in life. If that means anything."

Her words did not match her tone.

"Is there you something you'd like to say, ma'am?" he said.

She stared. "Only if there's something you want to hear."

The man shifted the gun over a few inches, the barrel against his breast. "Well you are certainly asking a lot of questions."

Denise grabbed a cold cup of coffee from behind the dresser and took a sip. "There's no real harm in being friendly."

"Only if the motivations aren't as holy as the words themselves," he replied, leaning in.

"Well then, do you want to know the truth?" she asked.

"Yes," he said, smiling sardonically.

"The truth is, mister," she said, and then added in a tone far less polite, "the truth is you have a gun in that jacket."

The man's smile faded.

"What's that?" he said.

"I said you have a small shotgun in that jacket," she replied.

"And what makes you think that?"

"I know. Just like I know that you don't do this very often. Just like I know plenty of things that nobody speaks of. You're trying to rob us. You think that we have money here. You've heard about the safe in the back and what's inside it, and you want it for your own."

Silence.

"We're good people," she added, "and we don't want any trouble. We never have."

The man leaned forward and whispered, "Forgive my manners, but I'm the one with the gun, ma'am."

She smiled, and then leaned in closer, bringing her voice to a cold monotone. "You're also the one who doesn't know what my husband packs in his back pocket everyday."

They both stayed silent for some time.

"It would be wise of you to leave," she added.

She stared back at the man and there was not a word between them. Even when Marcus stepped back into the room they didn't seem to notice. He ambled forward with a sense of hesitancy, three sandwiches in his hand, and to the man he offered only one.

"Marcus," his wife said, "I think you should give them to the man. It is a long ride to California."

The man took the gift and nodded but his eyes had not left the woman's and hers had not left his own.

"Bathroom. Where's the bathroom?" he said, almost inaudibly.

"In the back of the store," she replied.

The man turned in silence and walked into the rear as slowly as he could. From behind him both Marcus and Denise watched with measured trepidation.

The man slammed the bathroom door behind him. There was no way now. The man had failed. He thought of his son, and he thought of his wife. His mind wandered to a dream that he had many times before. It began in the same place—in a tiny boat, drifting and rocking just off the mainland, the man paddling desperately to get back to the coast. From the stern he could make out his wife and his son standing on the coast, mouthing uncertain words with uncertain meanings. Their mirages were pale and grey and they appeared as lifeless as dolls. When he turned his head, there were a hundred other boats just like his, paddling towards the same place, splashing the water just as incessantly, creating a current too dangerous to sit in, and a tide too lethal to swim in, setting up the inevitable demise of all those involved. The man always woke up before the waves overtook his vessel. He wondered if tonight the dream would be different.

Inside the bathroom the man shook with rage, carefully enough to keep quiet. A tear drop drifted down his right cheek and he wiped it away shamefully. The shotgun in his parka punched against his breast but he could not bring himself to carry out the deed. He thought of his son and he thought of his wife. He thought of the long highway ahead of them.

That's when he heard the voices.

He knew for certain by the creak of the door that someone else had stepped inside. He could make out three new sounds, quiet and faint, all of them men, and he heard a question asked about whether anyone else was there. He cracked the door open gently and caught a glimpse of a man, a hideous scarred man, dressed in all black, his hair greasy and sprayed in various directions, his face monstrous. The man shut the door hesitantly and leaned back onto the mildewed wall. From inside, he could hear everything.

"Do you own this store?"

"How'd you get this place?"

"Did you inherit it?"

"How'd a couple of animals like you end up on the upside?"

"Are you Christian niggers at least?"

He could have stepped out and started shooting but he was unsure how many men there were, let alone what they were carrying. Before long, Marcus's voice grew panicked and high-pitched and Denise began to scream. The man heard the tear of cloth and the sound of her clothes being ripped open, and then he closed his eyes as the noises became more and more grotesque. Marcus's cries, reduced to whimpers, gave way to the cacophony of his wife's screams, almost overshadowed by swine-like grunts and the audible violence of forced violation. The gunshots were unbearably loud and then there was a gurgle and a thud.

Silence now.

Many minutes came to pass before the man re-emerged. The store was quiet, inside at least, and within the confines of the aisles and refrigerators and ATM's, he saw nothing. Yet outside Marcus and Denise's car had been engulfed in flames, and another car was hurtling out of the station, roaring off into the night. Against the backdrop of the fire the sun had begun to vanish and the shadow of the evening loomed proudly. The crackle of combustion drowned out the dirge-like drone of the night's first crickets and cicadas.

Inside, the soda fountain was wholly intact, the junk food locked in place, exactly where it had been before. No freezer doors opened, no beef jerky sprayed out in the back aisles. If another person had entered at this point, it would have been just as standard as it had been five minutes before, just as distant and silent and predictable. The man walked to the front of the store, and that's when he saw the bodies.

Near the front entrance, the counter-top was sprayed with blood. Skull and brain tissue were painted onto the wall behind where the couple had stood only a few minutes before. He found Marcus dead, behind the register, blood running like a hose out from what the man presumed to be a gaping hole in the back of his head. He walked over to Marcus' corpse and leaned down, feeling his back pockets and finding nothing, no gun, no knife. The woman had lied. He turned to face her.

Denise lay nude and disgraced, covered in fluids, spread out on the floor in front of the gum rack. Maroon pooled around different sections of her figure. One cheek had been completely shot off, and there were scratches and cuts and scrapes over her entire body.

But she was alive, her chest heaving, her larynx wheezing and gurgling. The man made his way over to where she lay.

"The code," the man said, pulling the shotgun from his parka and pointing it at her corpse. "Give me the code for the safe."

"You," she choked out.

"The code," he said.

"You," she repeated, hacking and wheezing.

"Give me the code, Denise."

She shook her head.

"What's the point?" She spit up blood and three lines of it ran down her cheeks.

"There's no gun, there's no nothing, Denise. You lied. Do you hear me? You lied. Give me the fucking code."

She smiled, her last voluntary muscle function before her body began to seize. She coughed and choked and tears ran down her cheeks as her heart issued its final palpitations.

"Denise," the man said, his voice trembling, his eyes welling.

She could not respond, her body twitching and convulsing pathetically.

There was a pause as the two considered each other for the last time. The man pulled the trigger and she was gone.

Two hours later, the man returned to the motel room no wiser than when he had left, no richer either, his body sore and tired from the road.

The night was deep and silent and his wife he did not bother to rouse. His son almost immediately began to cry and he picked the baby up, offering him a piece of roast beef from one of the sandwiches, but the boy was too young to chew properly. Eventually the child went quiet, so the man laid him down to rest for the night and undressed his own body, piling his clothes by the air vent and stepping into the shower. The water ran a frothy pink down the drain and the porcelain was splashed with violet. After he had dried off, he redressed and paced himself to a bench outside the motel room door.

Sirens passed, portents of an insoluble future.

Later that night, the man sat in the local dive, a whiskey at his hands and a cigarette hanging limply from his lips. The man thought of his son, and after a moment he resigned himself to continue, as he had done countless times before. To his right sat the man with the scars, dressed in all blacks, his hair greasy, his face monstrous. Between them there was no threat of action, as both men remained unaware of the other's significance, the scarred man having never ever seen the other, and the other man being too drunk to even look up. The man with the scars picked pieces of tortoise shell from his boot heels and flicked them onto the ground aimlessly. No one prompted him a question, but he responded nonetheless.

"Nothing changed," he said.

Room 14
CHRISTIAN RILEY

Creatures of Habit

Roughly fifty miles northwest of Interstate 70, smack-dab in the heart of Middle America, sits a quaint and peculiar little town known as Ashbury. And within this town, believe it or not, live some very quaint and peculiar people who engage in the even more peculiar--albeit morbid--habit of eating the eyeballs of their citizens.

Of course, you won't notice those black gaping pits where such local's eyes once prevailed upon first glance, as you arrive upon that quaint little town. The scars left behind by their habitual appetites will most certainly be covered up with tinted spectacles, as you observe only the cozy features of the surrounding architecture, or perhaps even the vague hustle common with many other small towns, as laid out there in the streets before you. Or, if you're anything like me, you'll just be swept up by the warm smiles of those folks as they make their way along sidewalks and storefronts, while your VW van sputters into a broken heap on the side of the road. Still, whatever the case may be, rest-assured you'll feel right at home when you first enter into Ashbury, Middle America.

However, if you should succumb to any measurable length of stay in that town, if you are forced to seek some type of indoor service, where people tend to remove their shaded garments in pursuit of physiological relief, it won't be long before you discover that dismal custom of eyeball consumption, as practiced by those people of Ashbury. In fact, your first conversation with a person in that town may certainly provide for you your first clue, should you peer into their fleshy, forever lubricated empty eye-sockets.

At first, you'll think you've run across a human anomaly. Some poor soul who's obviously had an uncommonly rough life growing up in that charming little piece of America. You'll certainly ponder such notions as you gather what information you need from this individual, then carry on about your way. But eventually, you'll meet a second person from this town. And a second person will be all it takes for you to realize that the people of Ashbury seem to be infected with some kind of debilitating condition. A type of activity, or birth-defect that ultimately deprives them of their visual organs.

14

Or so you'll think.

This discovery will certainly stir your curiosity—again, again, if you're anything like me. So it's recommended that at this juncture, you visit any one of the few local diners in town. There, in those musty grease havens is where you'll find the ol' crows responsible for "cheffing" things up amongst their citizens. Look for the ones perched on a barstool, sipping coffee, as those are the guys you'll want to talk to.

A word of caution here, though—it won't be easy. First, you'll need to *woo* them with flattery, before those characters start coughing up some of their town secrets. Before they "get on" with why their palates prefer the taste of the human eye. And initially, the best way to achieve this—so I've found—is to pretend they don't even exist at all. Picture in your mind, if you will, the advice wilderness guides often give to hikers regarding the uncertain event of running across a grizzly bear, as you walk into one of those diners. Don't turn your back and run, yet be careful not to be so bold as to stare them in the face. Just act, for all intents and purposes, as if that thousand pound creature wasn't even there.

Now, although the people of Ashbury certainly aren't as dangerous as a grizzly bear (well, presumably so), the point here is to get their guards down, because understand this: to a town full of blind folks who can't see shit...any stranger who comes stumbling into their diner will be the one who sounds like a thousand pound grizzly bear, crashing through a campsite uninvited.

Half-way through your burger, one of those ol' crows will eventually say something to another. This'll be the first "casual" word spoken, since you rattled their cage by walking into that place. It'll be a mundane comment for sure, probably something about the weather; but in truth, it'll be a blind man reaching over with his long tongue, trying to get a sense for what you taste like.

Don't be alarmed though, 'cause this is a good thing. This means that you will have sparked their curiosity about you, and that now they're getting "itchy" about who this stranger in their diner is, eating one of their burgers (they are, after all, only human), and that you've been successful with your first task of ignoring them. Also, this will be the first sign of them letting their guards down, and so now you'll be at a crossroads to your quest.

Really know yourself before you make your next move here,

though. Really know what kind of person you are before you open your mouth, because I promise you, as blind people are wont to own a seemingly unnatural mastery over their remaining senses, those crows in that diner will smell any falseness in your voice as sure as the sun will set in that town. And if that happens, well...you might as well pack-up your shit and leave.

It might help if you consider the theory that there are two types of people in this world: those who rarely speak, and those who rarely shut-up. And although I believe that either one of those individuals could alas become successful at this point in time, within that diner, it is from the former in which I relate my experience to. But let me just add here that that too is good thing, because when you consider also the theory that those who rarely shut-up, rarely know how to listen, and therefore, rarely know how teach as well, then you'll recognize the fortune of having someone such as myself act as the purveyor of how to discover why the people of Ashbury are so inclined to gobble up their own eyeballs. So I'll say again...know what type of person you are before you speak.

Upon the utterance of that first casual word there in that diner, you may jump right in and follow suit with the topic at hand, if that's the type of person you are. But understand that by doing so, you'll also be *exposing* yourself to those folks of Ashbury; therefore, you will then have every tongue in that restaurant forgoing their apple pie while they lick the hell out of you. So the advice I prefer to give, upon hearing that first casual word, is to simply smile, nod in agreement, and then promptly pass your compliments from the waitress to the cook about how that just might be the best burger you've ever tasted in your life. To be sure, those crows in that diner will certainly salivate over that one.

Now at this point, if you're lucky, one of the bolder ones might just come right out and ask you, "Where you from, boy?" Or, you might hear something to the effect of, "Ain't they got good burgers where you's from?" (Of course, that last statement will be a deceptive play at modesty on their part, since no one in Ashbury contains an iota of doubt that such a fantastic burger may exist beyond the borders of their town). But if you're not so lucky as to have one of them ask you such a gorgeous, open-ended question like where you're from, or what kind of burgers you're used to tasting, then just hang in there; you've still got a piece of pie and

16

several cups of coffee waiting for you.

Assuming you've stayed the course in preserving such an innocuous manner about yourself, such an insipid flavor to that one long tongue which has been wandering through the crevasses of your ear since you've walked into that place, eventually one of those ol' crows won't be able to contain their curiosity anymore. And so, right about at the time when you're oohing and awing and making best friends with both the waitress and the cook because now you're eating the best piece of rhubarb pie you've ever had, well then, that's when one of those geezers will start squawking at you. Here is when you'll definitely be asked one of those beautiful questions, so be prepared to "play the game," as it were. And with that, of course, I now hand to you the most treasured piece of advice you'll need for this point in time within that diner: Bitching.

Almost as much as the taste of their own eyeballs, those folks of Ashbury love to bitch. In fact, once they get going, you'll hear nothing *but* bitching--all about anything and everything under the sun. But more specifically, (and most importantly, as you will see), they just love to bitch about "things not from Ashbury." Things which taste bad to them, or at the very least--*insipid*. Things which you and I are quite accustomed to ingesting; but, for the purpose of understanding why those people in that town have embraced that gruesome little habit of theirs, these should also be the same things which you find difficult to bare with anymore. Things which you feel are slowly poisoning you from the inside out, and are therefore *most worthy* of bitching about by even yourself...if you take my meaning.

No matter what kind of character you are, I promise you that this will be much easier than it sounds. And once you start bitching about all-that-you-know to those haggard magpies of Ashbury, and once they chime in with your efforts, guiding you along that track of complaints enhanced by their raspy snickerings, opening up to you because now they think you're alright, and because of this, they've let their guards way down, well...you'll swear you actually even *heard* the busting of that dam as it now lets loose a torrent of gossip there in that diner. A torrent of gossip...and other things.

So grab your seat, 'cause here it comes.

Remember to stay calm while those folks of Ashbury reveal to you a plethora of recipes in which they choose to fix-up their own eyeballs. Keep in mind, you're gonna hear all sorts of techniques and arguments over the proper preparation of their favorite delicacy, and you'll discover that some of them even have catchy names for a few of their dishes; such as: *Fried Eye Cream, Grilled Pear and Rosemary "Orb" d'oeuvres,* and *Rollie-Pollie Casserole.* I believe my favorite might have been *Marble Stew.*

Somewhere during all of this, you're also gonna hear a detailed description of when those folks decide the time is right for a "plucking." When they determine that an individual of their town has come of age, sort to speak, and that now their eyeballs are ripe for the taking. Almost always, as they explained to me, those eyeballs ripened up at around the age of fourteen. But every once in a while, there were a few which required harvesting at a much earlier age. Widely considered to be a true anomaly (if there ever was one), the flavor encompassed within those special jellies is just "...simply divine!" as a particular blind-man remarked to me.

In any case, what will eventually become apparent to you, while in that diner, is that the people of Ashbury are quite passionate about this epicurean habit of theirs. Without exception, each of them are connoisseurs of their own design, and despite what you, me, or anyone else thinks about the prospect of dining on a human eyeball, those particular folks of that quaint little town simply won't have things any other way.

Now, if you're a smart person, at this point you'll definitely pick up on *why* those people in that town have come to favor such cannibalistic tastes. (And once again, if you're anything like me, you'll also be ready to go check on your van, hoping it's fixed by now so you can hightail it out of there). However, if you still haven't yet discovered the truth behind why those folks of Ashbury consume the eyeballs of their citizens, then just relax, because it's likely that by now you'll also be on good enough grounds to just come right out and ask them.

This does, by the way, remind me of another thing I forgot to mention. Some point within that diner, while you're talking to those folks of Ashbury, and they're foaming at the mouth, confessing to you the rapture one receives from eating all those eyeballs, you're gonna start to wonder about your own little

18

spectacles--seeing as you still have them. And, you're also gonna wonder if *they're* wondering about them as well. But please be advised, just skip over this particular detail when it does occur in your mind. Because I'll tell you right now, that when a person gets older, the flavor of their eyes tends to fall...sour. Or so I've been told. It's a bad topic to bring up anyhow (unless of course, you're actually considering the prospect of "going blind"), as it will most certainly create for an awkward moment between you, and those old-timers of Ashbury.

There's one last thing I should offer you though, before I finalize this tale. As interesting as a trip through Ashbury may seem to be, with its quaint features, and *peculiar citizens*...there is a bit of harm which could fall upon you, if you should fail to take a certain precaution or two. Don't just hop into your car and peal out of that town once you suddenly get the urge to do so. But instead, take a minute to drive through the southern end of Ashbury, turning left at the corner where the firehouse is. Down that street lies a quaint little park teeming with kids, most of whom still have their eyeballs intact, and therefore, can still see things quite clearly. Take a slow drive past that place, making sure to catch a few of those stares from them *youngin's* as you do. Now I know that this advice might come across as being somewhat of a silly notion to you, but I'd also wager that if the last thing you picture in your head as you drive out of that quiet little town of Ashbury, is a flock of old fools in a fit of gluttony over a bowl of eyeballs...then it's likely that you'll *also* be left with a real nasty flavor in your mouth. A nasty flavor that just might render a certain "craving" of its own, as you grow older.

Room 20
DECLAN TAN

The Enigma of Hector Hauser

Not in the habit of going out much, he clumsily strangled the handle of the porch door to pull its mouth open. It swung tongue into carpet silence. At least, though he felt the face-wash of cliché, this is what he imagined to have happened. In 'truth' he did not actually know whether or where he had actually entered the pub to begin with, as memories of doors and windows had long since eluded his pitted mind. But he found himself in there anyway, sitting at the bar propping up his small head on his smallish hands, not crying, like pimiento in an olive.

He gummed the lips and the teeth, and the gums, of course, with a wet saliva kiss that tasted a bit like a cigarette sealed with last night's wine, that was both sweet and sick, a flavour that reminded him of the time he vomited after smelling the rank odour of cider-shit left in a friend's toilet one morning, after he had crashed squinting head backwards on the couch. When he had smelt it he had had to move quickly out through his friend's big front door to splash bile on the driveway. His friend did not like this (though it was his friend's fault, in many ways) because his friend would be forced to clean up after his guest at some later date. His friend could not do it immediately because they then went breakfasting together and did not return to the house for another two days. But this is part of the story not really worth telling. It bores me to remember it.

So as he was gumming his mouth, like an old man that's just tasted something he suddenly knows is 'off', he looked across the bar at another man, a really real one, not much different from any other whom you may find behind a bar at a certain clock hand of an evening, who was perusing his foreign newspaper. The bar tender, that was what he was, or at least had been identified as at the time.

Now. He is in Germany, a well-known but quite compact city known as Nuremberg, so things are a little different there. There they have bread named after elementary particles, which also happen to share the name of a mysterious yoghurt-like substance. Strange, up-down things. And, being in Germany, he would have to address the man formally with niceties; otherwise he may be at risk of squandering said Barman's good graces. But I'll translate for you, because it's easier that way.

Now again. I should also mention that at this time, to the right of our hero, there is a faceless man eating his dinner, seated at a table reasonably far off into the corner and with the front of his head facing the other way, at the wall. He seems to be forking the food in without hindrance; so we can suppose he has a mouth, at least. But you never know, he may be simply scooping the potatoes and gravy down the front of his shirt which is, of course, also a possibility, though probably a quite preposterous one. A fly is at his ear.

Back to our hero who, to his brothers at least, is known as Hector. This is because he works, during the day, as a ticket inspector. And you see, the two words rhyme. Yes, they do, don't they?

So. The Barman, who is also perhaps the proprietor of the deceptively large pub, with its backroom for pool and darts and a second bar for locals, is sat reading his paper, which is laid out across the entire width of the bar. He is only staring at the one page, and has been for quite a while, so maybe he isn't even reading it. But like Faceless, he at least appears to be doing what I said he was doing.

Hector at the bar: "'Scuse me. My name's Hector and I appear to be lost."

Barman doesn't look up. He's still ogling the sports section. Something about the Champions League.

After a moment, enough time to finish a sentence, a long one with pauses for effect, Barman's fingers tap on the bar next to where his paper's laid out. 'Right then,' his fingers seemed to say with their tiny fingertip mouths, 'What can I get you?' A friendly enough gesture indeed. Nothing out of the ordinary in a pub, German or otherwise.

"Um, I guess I'll have a pint." One second. "D'you have lemonade?"

Two seconds. No answer. He assumes there is none.

"Right, okay." He says, accepting the lemonade situation snappier than most backflip. But a twist of lemon is nice though, isn't it? If we're being honest. What sort of pub doesn't have lemonade, he's wondering. 'Strange German places these, aren't they?' he thinks to himself, idly. Hector's problems don't seem so much as problems to him by this time though; in fact he is quite content. So he can take the lemonade situation on the chin.

Barman doesn't move from his seat but instead reaches under the counter for a glass, probably not clean, and distractedly pulls the pint without looking. He keeps staring at the paper but we both know that he isn't reading it, he's just pretending. You can tell from the lack of focus in his little black eyes, he's watching in his periphery for the movement of the pint and/or Hector, our hero.

Hector spends the next few minutes quietly drinking his pint, occasionally looking around and then gumming like before, as if really tasting the barrel but liking it.

The pub from the inside is dark, there are booths and chairs and tables about, and the other things you usually find in a pub, even a German one which happen to be more like bars, just that everything in this one is dimmer by a few clicks. It contrasts the outer which is illuminated by what seems to be several streaming searchlights from up above. Strange, incoherent, confusing German places where people wait for the red man to turn into a green one.

Hector had heard crime rates were extremely low in that city but the evidence in the sky seemed now to prove to the contrary. He drinks his drink as the searchlights search, perhaps for people walking when the man stands red.

He finishes.

"Right so," Hector says (in German).

Not a peep. Same page. Champions League semi-finals. Barman immovable.

"Sounds like rain out there doesn't it? And what are all these searchlights about?"

He says, knowing silence will be his only reply. "Sounds pretty heavy that rain," he says then, urging something, even sort of looking in the direction of Faceless, probing for a response and hoping the potato-gravy-beef mouth isn't too full to gurgle words. It seems to be though, unfortunately, because there is only the sound of rain and window. The fly no longer at the ear.

"Well, if I have to stay here I'll guess I'll have another."

Two seconds. Two, two and a half, maybe. It doesn't really matter.

"How about something a bit more special?" The voice comes now, for the first time, as if from nowhere, as if from god or someone fatter, heavy with jumpy phlegm that has formed into a ball at the pit of the wide man's throat, sat there awaiting its purpose, much like the man who houses it, who is also a bit of a ball-shaped, phlegmatic thing.

Welcome, Hector is thinking, welcome to the conversation. Now he is just thankful for some vague communication that finally seems to be going somewhere.

"Sure, what've you got?" (He'll take anything).

Barman only gets up at this point and doesn't say anything else, his eyes, eyes like pinkies jabbed into Play-Doh, still entranced on the paper even though he's standing now. He leans over slightly, puts the used glass under the bar and, hunching at the shoulders, taps the wood where the drink once was, but this time it's different, the tapping; more urgent. A money request. Hector takes out the coins from his pocket and lays a few of them down, enough to cover two drinks. Barman taps again, slower, heavier like his fingers are growing thicker. Hector puts down another coin, a silvery one. Another tap. A gold one. It keeps going like this until all the coins are on the bar, even the little ones that Barman doesn't like. Barman collects.

As he walks off he keeps his tiny eyes on the line in that paper, even as he moves off. Ridiculous. He puts his hands in his pockets and goes up the stairs toward the far end of the bar and finally gives up the pretence of looking at the paper when his head disappears up the stairway; his head that is thinking about Schalke and the 1934 Final and beating Nuremberg, 2-1. Sweet beershit victory.

Hector is now looking at the Faceless Man, for some explanation, some reasoning, or something. Because it all seems a little odd, even for a bar in Nuremberg. Germany's safest of cities, to his mind. Faceless is still forking though, paying no attention. Just eating away at his dinner that doesn't seem to end. Fly back at the ear?

Barman comes back and as soon as we can see his eyes again they're back on that line, back in that paper, his balding head doing what it does. Schalke: unbeaten 1935–1943, he's thinking. Barman comes back with nothing in his hands and takes his seat and sits lurched there all over again.

'€6.80,' he's thinking. 'Where's my €6.80?' Questions like these. 'That was my last six Euros and eighty cents.' Quite baffled he stands there waiting.

"How about that drink then, hum?"

Barman gets up. Barman goes over to Faceless and talks to him while Hector tries to listen. He can't hear the words but thinks it too impolite to approach, plus he's a little frightened of seeing a man with no face, and gravy all over it. There are only a few words exchanged, nothing really to speak of, except that they are the only words either two of them have spoken to each other so far. Which makes them somehow significant. More beams of light outside, the weather howling wolf.

Barman comes back; he seems to be the landlord of the pub so any complaints will have to be taken up with him.

Hector eyes Landlord, sitting there with his new title that he has earned via syllogistic evidence. Hector has slightly bigger eyes than he though, and feels mighty good about it. Despite the imbalance of property ownership.

"Yeah, how about that drink then? Where's that something special?" (In German).

"I have no idea what you're talking about, sir." (Also in German, formal).

"I gave you €6.80 for a drink. Something special you said. Then you went upstairs."

"I really have no idea what you're talking about, sir,' says the Landlord. 'Captain. Do you know what's he talking about?"

The back of the Faceless man's head shakes side-to-side, quite eerily and murderously slow.

"See. We don't know what you're talking about."

"Look, I gave you…" Hector's hand goes into the pockets to show that it's empty, that he gave him all he had. But of course the money comes pouring out onto the hardwood floor. He can tell quite quickly, with the gold coins and the silver coins and the little ones that no one likes, that it amounts to roughly, perhaps exactly, six Euros and eighty cents. Dull coins that have lost their shine. Hector the Inspector gets a feeling of dread.

He sits down and thinks, looking out at the searchlights still searching and, through the translucent windows, sees them getting closer, more interested in the pub. The single glaze kind of rattles with the wind and rain; the kind of windows that close or open with no one around doing it. He feels slightly irked. The coins are still on the floor.

He takes a bow and picks them up, sometimes one at a time, sometimes pinched fingerfuls. He has a little trouble getting at some of the ones glued to the sticky floorboards.

That voice from over the bar, at the crouched Hector: "How about a drink then?" It feels a bit like pity with that tone and that formal register.

"Yes." Three seconds. "OK." Another drink.

Landlord is looking at him as he pulls the pint and as Hector stands up. Both pairs of eyes go straight past each other and through the other's sockets into dark skulls. The pint is creamy. The pint is drunk. Tap on the table; money needed. The weather worsens and searchlights shine, on occasion, directly through the stained glass back and forth from the well-kept, orderly countryside of Germany.

"Do you have any rooms here?" Rooms to sleep in, rooms to rest his small head and smallish hands.

"Do you have any money?" Money for drinks, money to pay for rooms, money for rooms to rest his small head, smallish hands.

"None. No, wait. I have some, don't I?" He smiles the first uneasy smile of many and sprinkles those coins down.

Landlord sits back on the stool, looks at the paper, reads the words. Hector sips. Hector wants to cry. He is finished.

"How much for a room, then?"

"Oh." Conversation is coming easy now. "Don't worry about that. You can go right up."

"What room, where is it?"

"There is only one room."

A nod from Hector as if to say 'Of course there's only one room. And it probably has a 'K.' on the door.' He looks at the pint but remembers he has no more of the six Euros and eighty cents. The money appearing and reappearing. Sometimes more, sometimes less. At this point: €6.79.

In the morning, it is still dark. As dark as last night. He gets up off the thin mattress and goes downstairs in a somnambulant daze, rubbing his eyes, as you do.

A man with his back turned to the bar is eating gravy and potatoes and slices of beef. For Hector, he has no face. A ball of a man, balding, is at the bar reading the paper. The weather outside is strange: spotlights and searchlights and beams of whatnot light the outer windows, windows translucent, windows that silhouettes may stand behind, in the right conditions, in the wrong story.

Hector is afraid to go outside, so he takes a stool, a different one to last night, more directly in front of Barman and he plops down.

"How about a drink, then?" Hector says, somewhat bored. He feels like crying somehow, but he can't.

Barman looks up. He says, "How about something special?"

Hector drops the coins again, seeing where this is going.

Six Euro coins; eighty single cent pieces.

Hector sighs, fakes his next smile, and carefully peels off the sunken features of his soon-forgotten face.

Room 27
JASON PRICE EVERETT

Sepsis

The itch was maddening. Evenings he would tear off his socks and claw at it until the blood came but nothing worked. The exposed surface reminded him of certain desert succulents, the submerged flesh smooth and glistening. There was no pain, just the itch. He broke his fingernails in the tender quick of his instep.

The first time he saw the whiteness it took him all of a minute to realize that it was in fact a sliver of bone. He touched it with curiosity. It felt like plastic, like the handle of a hairbrush. The itch was behind the bone, inside the handle. With a flash of fear he went to work.

Armies of intent mites, red and black, streamed from his gestating marrow. He would crush them in droves. Their liquefied bodies smeared his hands, streaked his arms, daubed his face. His feet were ruins. He snapped the stumps of his carpals like overworked pencils and threw them across the room. The insects grew wings and flew away. An unfamiliar species of worm replaced them. Their eggs were like grains of rice. Their interior was grey. His own substance seemed to have been entirely consumed by his new inhabitants. It didn't hurt at all.

The lower half of his bed was a sodden shipwreck of blood, ichor, scraps of flesh and bone splinters. His dirty covers saturated, he threw them away. The mattress was stained beyond salvage.

He wandered his room, rubbing the tottering stumps of his ankles against any sharp edge that might present relief to the burning itch. He rubbed himself away upon his furniture and accomplished nothing more than his own erosion.

One hand scratched the other into nonexistence. His teeth chewed his restless tongue into vibrating shreds of separate irritation. The inside of his mouth writhed with subcutaneous movement. Interlocking surfaces grew from pinpoints into irregular sores, linked, spread, dilated and thinned into curtains that shed their shredded strands in the wind of his exhalations.

Exhausted, he lay unmoving in the morass of his body. The itch was all that remained. Waves of the itch marched at intervals through his ragged tenement of a body. He picked idly at an exposed rib. He plucked it. It made a surprisingly pleasant sound. Expectorating wet laughter he tuned up and down the smeared cage of his inborn instrument. When all the ribs that he could reach had snapped from the tension he stopped. The tune that he had played was of necessity unaccompanied and wordless.

The bunker of his skull evacuated legions of small scavenging things. His remains settled into a small pool of flavorless fluid. Its clear surface would not admit of more than a minute ripple or two. Sometimes two of the ripples would intersect.

A rain of condensation from the ceiling turned the pool into a garden of expanding concentric circles.

Room 29
JAMES H. DUNCAN

The Captain

the driver of the greyhound bus stares
over us like a prison guard might,
the look of disdain and long silence,
and yes, we are the rabble, wards
of an uneasy state, surrogates of an
unwelcome future, and we come from
the broken city of fractured, limping
souls, the leeches of Manhattan, the
ineffectual Prometheans of Brooklyn,
the wretches of Queens and dim flickering
lights of Long Island and New Jersey,
we are his carriage, his cargo, his crew,
and he is the Captain, the worst fumbling beetle
of us all, trolling the same pockmarked route
over and over in his flagging blue uniform

let him stare at us with his dour eyes;
we are exactly as he sees us, which is more
than he can say for himself when he wakes
and washes his face before the mirror each
and every harrowing day of his endless
life, which will, of course, end in the same
flameout way we all will, with our backs
against the wall, darkness for sight, and a
skeletal hand lighting our last cigarette
before the sound of the highway comes back
to our ears, reminding us of all the miles and the
routes not taken, and then—the final bullet's cry

JAMES H. DUNCAN

The Rotting Stage

Joseph writes plays about talking
squirrels in central park and their
Communist takeover of the merry
-go-round, terrorizing children
and hot dog vendors alike, and he
talks a good game of anti-government
damn-the-man heroism, but really…
what does it all matter if we all file
by the 15th, and we all like Guinness,
and we all wear thick cotton socks,
and we all have a mother who loved
us at least until she got to know us

Joseph says he write about truth through
the absurd, but what happens on his stage
never make as much sense as what
happens in the dark of your room at night,
with all the razor blades whispering from
beneath the mattress, a chorus line of hope

Room 31
TOM VICK

Crepuscule Junction

Things were different back then. Back then a man could head west with nothing but the shirt on his back and a heart full of determination and make something of himself. He could strike out with nothing but the shirt on his back, a heart full of determination, a bunch of law books and maps, a few pints of good whiskey, some expensive cigars, a generous supply of cash and a pragmatically pessimistic view of the human nature, and make his mark on posterity.

Those were the days of handshake deals and gentlemen's agreements, when a man could walk into the office of a smalltime state legislator, let's say, and just spend the afternoon shooting the breeze, man to man, over cigars and whiskey, followed by a night on the town, funded by the visitor's generous supply of cash (which by the next morning the legislator – waking up in his underwear in a strange room with a pummeling hangover, and are those a pair of stockings draped over the lightshade? – will not be able to recall) and get what he came for: a little piece of land, nothing special, situated at a t-shaped intersection out in the middle of nowhere, a ghost town, really, with a few abandoned buildings here and there that most people might not even notice if they happened by. For most men, as we know, are easily bought. Their desires are simple: liquor, women, money, tickets to sporting events, and these things have not changed over time, over the centuries.

This is how Dan Bedloe, in 1953, founded the city of Crepuscule Junction.

All that matters to us is that it started at a horse racing track back east. Rail thin, wraithlike, of indeterminate middle age, Bedloe would later appear in the memories of the other track regulars as some kind of ghost, an unfocusable image of a man who existed once, somehow, in the periphery of their vision, on the edges of their liquor-and-gambling besotted lives, who maybe once in a while now shows up in dreams or in the faces of similarly-featured men seen on the street or in passing cars: dried-up, determined, unapproachable-looking men probably on a mission of some kind.

No record of Bedloe's life exists before his time at the track, so we can imagine him simply appearing, spending nearly every day there, quiet, keeping to himself, a disciplined and meticulous player of horses with an arcane and remarkably successful system for interpreting the endless columns of tiny numbers printed on betting sheets, possessed of an admirable self-discipline that allowed him to keep his winnings rather than piss them away in the typical financial death spiral of the compulsive gambler. You would never have picked him out of the crowd of shriveled, hollow-eyed, chain smoking wrecks, religious in their reliance on superstition, fuzzy math skills and blind luck, the types that still populate that same track decades later, only now tied umbilically by credit cards on chains around their necks to bright and noisy slot machines, staring bloody-eyed at video screens in the colorfully lit interior gloom while the horses run the track outside to a meager audience of children and a dwindling handful of genuine racing enthusiasts.

We can imagine him materializing out of thin air among the throng of unnoticing bettors, just as, a few years later, he would seem to suddenly materialize in a police officer's uniform at a lonely crossroads out west.

After the plan formed in his mind he set a goal, the amount of money he would need to make it work, and once he'd won enough at the track he pulled up stakes and drove across the country over interstates whispering to him of endless possibility through the smooth thrumming of his tires on their still-new surfaces. Through the forests and hills of the east he drove, sharing the roads with vacationing families, fat with postwar prosperity in giant convertibles, smiling in the formation we are familiar with from vintage television commercials and photographs of old billboards: father and mother in the front, Bobby and Susie in the back, families with savings accounts, life insurance policies and mortgages. We can picture the highways full of them, smilingly driving. How he must have stood out, this quiet, thin, older man, always in a suit and tie, eating at diner counters, occasionally jotting something in a notebook. Would he have resembled, to them, a traveling salesman perhaps, that lost and mythical beast of the mid-20th Century? Those lonely, tired men, driving with their cases of samples, living out of motel rooms, drinking whiskey out of motel glasses, smoking unfiltered cigarettes, wearing undershirts and suspenders in the darkness of another dingy room in another little town, their suit pressed and ready for the morning rounds, during which they will transform themselves into charming, fast-talking and loquacious gentlemen, gentlemen who'll do anything to get a foot in the door.

There is a sad poetry to the very thought of them now, for they are gone.

In Bedloe's trunk, instead of sample cases, he carried a suitcase, law books and maps, the products of months of research, looking for the place to fit the idea in his head, a unique and impossible idea of a city in the desert, the germination of which we'll never know for his was a singular mind, watchful, calculating, perhaps possessed of a form of genius, at any rate undistracted by emotions, and able to hone in on exactly what would be required for his project.

In his mind was a t-shaped intersection, in the seeming middle of nowhere, but perfect for his plan based on his study of population projections, zoning laws, and a million other factors he sat figuring out in the course of his research, factors not even the people who calculated them knew or cared how to put together because they weren't thinking like he was, research as arcane as his system for betting on horses and akin to it because it involved pouring over what no one wants to bother to pour over, finding overlooked connections, the kind of project a man as gaunt, quiet, and nearly invisible as he was might naturally gravitate towards if he had such a mind as his.

Bedloe continued on across the Mississippi, across the tedious and wind-whipped prairie (where he lost his hat and had to buy a new one), and finally into that vast western landscape that has inspired so many, left them silent and stricken with awe. Finally he came to the t-shaped crossroads he had pinpointed, one tiny point in that vast flat landscape where one road, running north from the interstate, led to Fort Butte and some natural wonders just awakening to the phenomenon of tourism, beckoning to those smiling nuclear families, and another road ran east to the fast-growing town of Butte Fork. He already knew about the abandoned general store placed right at the intersection, and from maps he also knew the location of each of the few deserted houses scattered around the unincorporated area between the two Butte-named towns, the only nearby population centers.

It was that subtle gradation of twilight known as crepuscule when he arrived, for sunsets, especially in the west, are so spectacular that we feel compelled not just to name them but to name every part of them, every sliver of time, as if labeling each sinking instant will prolong them, make the evening ours forever. Now he could rest, and not lacking a hint of poetry within him, or discovering that hint now that he found himself in a landscape more awe-inspiring than his calculations and research could have possibly prepared him for, he dubbed the place, but only in his mind for now, Crepuscule Junction.

We can picture him sleeping a self-satisfied sleep in his car that night, under the millions and millions of stars. In the morning he awoke to the sounds of traffic whooshing by, and sweet to him was the sound. He counted the cars, made more notes and calculations in his notebook, and then what? Did he smile to himself? He must have. How could he not, even though he was not the smiling type, but even those types must smile sometimes when they are alone. He was new to this world, alone in a vast and craggy landscape punctuated by buttes, redolent of violence, almost still red with it, a land where marauding soldiers, guns for hire, rustlers and outlaws slaughtered the native population for food, sport and money not even a century ago, where toothless, bearded, unscrupulous men sometimes accompanied by thin-lipped women in bonnets and gaggles of dirty-faced children once bungled their way west in the clumsy expansion of this nation, and which was now a much more peaceable place, where people were just beginning to spend their evenings inside watching television instead of on the porch watching the sun go down, and where years later technology would allow them to take their TV's outside if they liked.

After buying the land and all the abandoned buildings upon it from the state, he moved into a back room of the dilapidated general store, and for three years seemed to hibernate there, to exist motionless like some kind of organism that remains dormant for years at a time and then emerges into the world according to the unfathomable inspiration of instinct, surviving, as he would tell his family later, on instant coffee, peanut butter sandwiches and cigarettes.

It was in 1953, three years after his arrival, that he paid another visit to the state legislator and officially incorporated his new town of Crepuscule Junction.

Shortly thereafter he returned to the legislator's office bearing again some of those treats to which men's simple weaknesses bend, and emerged this time with the even more important elements of his plan: a new traffic signal for the intersection at Crepuscule Junction, and along with it a police car and deputy's uniform tailored for his size, for Bedloe was a reasonable man, and concerned about public safety, so he had volunteered to police the intersection himself, asking only in return for the uniform and the car.

That's how things worked back then, when a man's word was a man's word, and a handshake meant something. A simpler time, uncomplicated, pure, honest and free. The America we look back on with nostalgia, uncorrupted, innocent, righteous and true.

Righteous and true and self-made American that he was, Bedloe, now in possession of a police car and a sheriff deputy's uniform, parked himself beside that intersection and began writing tickets, kicking some of the revenue back to the helpful legislator (for that was part of the deal) and keeping the rest for himself as mayor and sole resident of Crepuscule Junction.

And this is how the town grew. Bedloe converted the general store into the town hall, where he served as sheriff, traffic cop, mayor and head of the immediately created Crepuscule Junction Department of Motor Vehicles.

Imagine how surprised those first drivers were, first by the new traffic light in the middle of nowhere and second to be pulled over, even if they did stop for it, and issued tickets for such offenses as not stopping long enough or having a broken taillight, a slightly deflated tire or a dusty license plate. Pulled over by this rail thin, middle-aged cop who was just as friendly as could be and sincerely apologetic for having to do this, and who would send them off with a pleasant reminder to "drive safe, now."

The residents of Butte Fork and Fort Butte got the worst of it, forgetting as they did from day to day about the new development at the intersection. Some of them got several tickets in the first week. Bedloe even managed to take more than one tourist for multiple tickets in a single day by taking advantage of the similarity of the two towns' names. "Fort Butte?" He would say, "I thought you said Butte Fork. That's over that way, and by the way, I'm real sorry, but I noticed that your left rear tire is a touch underinflated. I really hate to do this, but I'm going to have to write you another ticket."

So you might say that Crepuscule Junction started out as a DMV office and a city grew up around it. But this was just one more facet of Bedloe's remarkable foresight. He had calculated the vectors of the new freeway system, saw that it would bring people closer than ever to the road between Butte Fork and Fort Butte, and forecast that those very interstates would in turn create the demand for more cars, all of which would mean more revenue for him. You might say that his DMV was the most thriving business in that part of the state, and yet Bedloe continued to live frugally in a back room, saving his money until he had enough to buy more and more parcels of adjoining land, later developing them into housing tracts and business areas, and those flush postwar families, drawn by the freeways and the fresh air, the lure of possibility, began to populate his city. By 1963 it appeared to be a town like any other. Once the population grew large enough, a local government was formed, with Bedloe, who made a point of getting to know everybody in town, elected mayor. The old abandoned houses were spruced up and turned into a historic district, with invented pioneer rituals performed on holidays, and the surrounding housing tracts multiplied, along with the businesses established to cater to the growing populace.

Sixty-some years after its founding on that abandoned stretch of road, people still spend most of their time at the DMV in Crepuscule Junction, which grew, over the decades, into a grand, proud bureaucracy housed in a palace-like building inspired by the pyramids of Mexico named the Dan Bedloe Memorial Department of Motor Vehicles Ziggurat, which sits on the very spot where the general store used to be, right in the center of town.

Nowhere in this troubled nation are the races, creeds and genders so united as when they suffer as one within the confines of the Crepuscule Junction DMV. How heartwarming it is to see blacks, whites, Asians, Native Americans and Latinos, old people and teenagers, Christians, Jews and Muslims, shaking their heads in commiseration together, and complaining in harmony as they wait in line for days only to be told that they need another form or a hundred more dollars to finish whatever transaction they are trying to complete. And that's just the information line.

The building's inner sanctum, a vast, high-ceilinged, echoing room surrounded by bulletproof glass behind which the clerks, imperiously and slowly, process transactions, is nearly always full to capacity with people from all walks of life, some of them in sleeping bags, having spent days waiting to be called to the windows, others meditating or praying. One wouldn't be surprised to see bony old men dressed in rags and sporting long white beards, begging for scraps of food, having grown ancient in that room waiting for a driver's license or a registration card. They say that no one promises more to God than the person who's drunk themselves sick, kneeling at the toilet heaving up the contents of their stomach, but whoever said that has never been to the Crepuscule Junction DMV on a busy weekday. People have been known to spend weeks extricating themselves from the byzantine, interlocking vehicle regulations that the DMV employees (the most handsomely paid sector of the city workforce) call, among themselves, Ouroboros: the world-encircling snake swallowing its own tail.

Now a model for DMV offices in cities across these United States, its success can be traced to the fact that over the sixty-odd years since its founding, Crepuscule Junction has grown into a diverse, thriving metropolis, growing like an organism from the Petri dish of Bedloe's traffic light. Housing developments spread in all directions. Commercial boulevards now stretch to the vast western horizon, lined with lighted signs for Pizza Hut, Motel 6, Walmart, Sunoco: jumbles of poles, each trying to reach higher than the next. By happy coincidence they look their best at crepuscule-time, when their glow begins to outdo that of the setting sun, and their colors become bold against the darkening sky. Among its many attractions, Crepuscule Junction boasts the largest rotating 76 Gas Station sign in the world. Rising above and dwarfing all signs around it (and kept that way by city ordinance), its orange orb turns hypnotically in the night, a beacon to travelers or, as some would have it, a warning sign to those unfortunate enough to have been snared by the ziggurat to turn around and head the other way.

Room 38
JOHN DORSEY

Convictions

when i was a kid
we didn't talk about my uncle jerry
coming home drunk with a gun to his head

we didn't talk about sex, drugs, or forgery
because my aunt darlene got sent away
for passing bad checks
after skipping town at 19
to marry a trucker
who stole my grandparents fine china
to buy a "lifetime supply" of pain killers
that lasted 2 days

we didn't talk about mental illness
even though my aunt victoria
used to snap rubber bands
against her wrists every time she felt sad
and my grandmother talked to butterflies
claiming they were my grandfather's spirit
she probably still does

we didn't talk about my brother's drug arrest
or how my dad had to become a cold empty vessel
just to stay sane
i don't blame him anymore

we didn't talk about the photo of me
with a joint in my mouth at the age of 3
taken in the bed of my uncle jan's pickup.

we didn't talk about how
my grandmother
was the product of rape

there was no sex, drugs, or forgery
just Kiss cranked up loud
coming from my aunt's bedroom window
and whispers about convictions
about pride
about a happy hour
that rarely came without red nosed guilt

when my grandmother finally told me
that my aunt got "sent away"
i asked if i could go too
as if she was at summer camp
writing us all a happy note
on the back of a norman rockwell postcard

i guess every family comes with its own rap sheet

someone once said that
blood is thicker than water

and that love can be a hard pill to swallow
unless you take it by the handful
and let it
sing you
to sleep

JOHN DORSEY

The strong silent type

after the reading
an old Ukrainian man
told me that what i needed was
a dirty dirty woman and pointed to my date
who broke down in tears

when we walked outside to smoke a cigarette
she told me about how she had been gang raped
in the woods by a group of neo-nazis
who had promised her a pot plant
when all she had ever really wanted
was for someone to legalize love

as we sat in her apartment filled with bibles
and every book allen ginsberg ever translated into hindu
and onto the unpaved streets of nirvana
she told me her life story in pig latin and air guitar
on an imaginary second hand gibson
that had more cracks in it
than her heart did

somehow she had managed to hide
dreams under her fingernails
as i looked outside her bedroom window
i noticed that her stars
were the strong silent type
like polished bone
like wisdom laid to rest
she could never go home

the next morning
half asleep, she told me
that her nightmares were proof
that you didn't have to be a ghost
to die inside

Room 41
GARRETT SOCOL

Strange Events of the Senior Year

There was no explaining the gruesome trend that grabbed hold of high school seniors in the small town of Solon Springs, Wisconsin smack in the middle of an unusually mild winter. One season earlier, national news was made by a rash of sophomore suicides that plagued a prestigious Ivy League university. Baffled parents in Wisconsin wondered if this had inspired their teenage children to devise their own original take on that morbid series of events.

Solon Springs was a miniscule microcosm compared to its nearest big city, Chippewa Falls. Named after French fur trader Daniel Greysolon Dulhut (who came from Montreal by way of the Great Lakes in 1680), it was a terribly scenic place dominated by towering pine trees. The town was home to Mom and Pop stores as opposed to chains and mini-malls, barber shops as opposed to beauty salons, and determined parents who were opposed to sending their children to out-of-state colleges.

The victim of the first shocking incident was Sherman Quisenberry, an above average student who worked part-time at the Dairy Queen and sang in the church choir. His body was discovered on a quarter-mile stretch of highway 53 that narrowed to a single lane going north and a single lane heading south. The Greyhound bus that struck him was travelling twenty miles per hour above the speed limit, but this seemingly significant fact didn't faze the citizens of Solon Springs. It was commonplace for anyone traversing that stretch of lonesome highway to exceed the speed limit.

Still, the tragedy was major news. Despite the fact that traces of marijuana were found in the boy's blood, the residents of Solon Springs mourned the loss of Sherman Quisenberry as if he'd been a member of their immediate family.

The next tragic incident occurred precisely ten days after the first. The body of Priscilla Swanson was discovered on the same desolate stretch of highway that claimed Sherman Quisenberry. Soft-spoken and shy, Priscilla loved hot cocoa, Elvis, and cutting herself. She had a habit of puncturing her pale skin, small areas on her arms and legs. She claimed these were accidental wounds but the wise kids suspected she was doing it on purpose. The Greyhound bus that ran her down had been roaring along the road at fifteen miles per hour above the speed limit.

Both Sherman and Priscilla were short, introspective, and didn't draw unnecessary attention to themselves (except when Priscilla displayed a new bandage), so when the body of the third victim, Andrew "Grunt" Galloway, was discovered ten days after Priscilla's, the authorities were confounded; this notorious "bad boy" didn't fit the mold. Cocky, tall and confident, he swaggered down hallways, skipped important tests and propositioned the babes who sometimes said yes. According to several colleagues, Grunt was always a little high, so it was no surprise that a large amount of marijuana was found in his system. The Greyhound bus that hit him had been zooming down Highway 53 at ten miles per hour above the speed limit.

There were only a handful of lampposts dotting that particular stretch of Highway 53, each exploding in a burst of yellow phosphorescence that almost seemed a waste of energy. Nothing grew, nothing thrived, there was no scenery to admire, not a solitary shrub. The light faded fifty feet from its source, allowing the darkness beyond to thicken and seem ominously alive. Only the moon, when it wasn't hidden by clouds, brightened the forgotten patches of road. After the third tragic incident, the region had undergone a major transformation; it resembled a veritable arboretum with roses, tulips, hydrangea, lilies and orchids lining the highway for what seemed like miles.

The town flew into an absolute frenzy when the body of Evan Smiley was found ten days after Grunt's. Evan was an outstanding student and an affable guy primarily known for his musical ability and garish socks. He taught himself how to play the piano and the guitar, and he was often asked to perform at local functions. The Greyhound bus that hit him had been moving down Highway 53 at five miles per hour above the speed limit. Traces of rum and Coke were found in his system. He was wearing bright orange socks with a navy blue butterfly pattern.

Teachers were instructed to discuss these tragedies in their classrooms. Parents were urged to speak candidly to their stunned teenage children, to remind them that suicide is a permanent solution to a temporary problem. A grief counselor from Madison was hired to appear at the high school every Monday and Friday. Black funeral dresses were in such demand that Ella of Ella's Boutique had run out. It became commonplace for small groups of women to drive to Chippewa Falls, enjoy a tasty lunch at Bridgewater Restaurant, and then shop for funereal garb at the popular Fashion Bug. They made an afternoon of it.

High school principal Sidney Tomkins called a special assembly, mandatory for all students. Standing on the stage of the auditorium, he read the mission statement of the Solon Springs Area Unified School District: "In partnership with the community, we are committed to excellence, empowering and challenging all students to learn while preparing them for an ever-changing global society." These words were met with scattered applause, mostly by teachers and cafeteria workers. Tomkins scanned the blank faces of the students. "If any of you is unhappy about something, my door is open. If you don't like the lunches we serve, if you think our fitness equipment should be upgraded, if you're having a problem at home, I'm available day or night."

"Fitness equipment?" Gail Reinjohn whispered to Marshall Calabrese who was sitting next to her in the back of the auditorium.

"Pathetic," Marshall replied. "He doesn't have a clue."

The principal continued. "You're at an age when you're trying to make sense of your life, and it doesn't make much sense, does it?" These words elicited a few tepid laughs. "But death is not an option. Even if your problems seem insurmountable, you have to face them. You can't decide to skip the hard part. The hard part is what develops character."

"Who developed *his* character?" Marshall whispered to Gail.

"They forgot to *give* him one," she whispered back.

When the assembly ended and the students began to disperse, Gail and Marshall decided to meet for a quick bite at six o'clock.

"The adults are in such shock," Gail said over a garden salad. "Did your parents talk to you?"

"Nah," he said over a well-done cheeseburger. "They never talk to me unless it's to stop practicing the trumpet."

"My mother asked me if I knew any of the kids," she said with incredulity. "The seniors at Solon Springs High are killing

43

themselves. I'm a senior at Solon Springs High. Does she think there are two million of us?"

"Did you tell her they were all in McKenna's class?"

"No."

"It's only a matter of time," Marshall said.

Gail found Marshall immensely attractive and entertaining, but she suspected he was gay. He never made a pass at her, didn't like football and ate low-fat yogurt. In any case, she felt safe and comfortable with him.

Ten days after Evan's body was found, the bodies of Melinda Early and Davis McCaffery were discovered side by side on Highway 53. This double suicide, the first of its kind in Solon Springs, stunned an already unnerved community. The two seniors had been dating for over six months and the relationship seemed to be getting serious. Rumors that Melinda was pregnant were quickly denied.

"They had their whole lives," Melinda's mother sobbed to a reporter. "I can't understand it."

"This has got to stop!" Elena Kroll declared to the rolling camera of the local news station. "We're losing our children and we don't know why. Someone has to know why. Whoever you are, please talk to us!" Elena's two daughters were only nine and seven, but she wanted this suicidal trend to stop before they entered their teens.

When Gail heard the news, she immediately called Marshall. "What's wrong?" he asked. "You sound terrible."

"I don't know if I can deal with this anymore," she said in tears.

"Meet me at the benches near the bookstore in ten."

"Fine," she told him. Even though she lived only five or six minutes from the bookstore, Gail grabbed her wool coat and headed out the door. She was restless; she couldn't sit still.

The air was cold. In fact, the temperature was the lowest it had been all winter. She reached for her gloves in the side pockets. The left glove was in the left pocket but the right pocket was empty. No glove. She looked behind her to see if it had fallen to the ground. She checked all pockets thoroughly. The right glove was gone and she was going to have to deal with it.

When she arrived at the benches, Marshall wasn't there, so

she paced. Back and forth, forth and back, from one tall pine tree to the next, about six feet apart. As she tried catching her breath, she imagined how her family would react to her suicide. Her parents would never get over it, Gail thought. They would be destroyed, haunted and pained for the rest of their lives. Her little brother wouldn't understand, but when he got older he would be deeply sorry he no longer had a sister to confide in.

Marshall walked quickly toward the pacing girl. "Hey," he said.

"Hey," Gail responded. "She was pregnant, you know."

Marshall stopped in his tracks. So did Gail. "I thought they said she wasn't."

"They said she wasn't, but she was. Janet Arliss told me. She was Melinda's best friend."

"Shit," Marshall whispered.

"Look, I don't believe a fetus is a baby," Gail stated with conviction. "A fetus is a fetus and a baby is a baby. But still, there was something growing inside her, and it was on its way to becoming a baby. And the notion of killing that along with herself is just overwhelming to me. I can almost understand how she could kill herself, but not the fetus."

"I hear you."

"This is insanity because I am so pro-choice. Why am I so upset?" she cried.

"You just are. We're all in a little bit of shock and we react in unexpected ways."

"I think I've lost my mind."

"You're just a little confused. We all are."

"What the hell is going on, Marshall?"

"I'm not sure. But it's pretty shitty." He took a deep breath, tried to focus. "How about a movie later?"

"I'm so not in the mood."

"That's exactly why we should go."

Light snow flurries began to fall while Marshall and Gail were in line for tickets at the local Cineplex. "In the middle of dinner last night," Marshall said, "my father said to me, 'Suicide is a permanent solution to a temporary problem. You know that, right?'"

"What'd you say?" she asked.

45

"I said, 'I didn't know that, but thanks.'"

"Did he realize you were mocking him?"

"I'm not sure. You have to keep in mind that my father's an idiot."

"Oh, OK."

"You feeling better?" he asked with hesitation.

"A little, I guess," Gail reported.

"Two for the Tarantino film," Marshall said to the balding man when they arrived at the ticket booth. Gail dug into her bag, but Marshall said, "I got it."

"Thanks," she replied. She honestly hadn't expect him to pay, and this made her wonder if Marshall was straight and this was an actual date.

When they sauntered into the theatre, the lights were still on and the screen was blank. "Where do you like to sit?" Gail asked.

"Aisle seat, like on an airplane."

They took two seats in the third to last row. "I prefer window," Gail offered.

"You want to move?" he asked with a straight face.

"I think all the window seats are taken."

"We could ask a flight attendant to see if anyone wants to switch."

"You say everything with such a straight face," Gail remarked. "Do some people think you're being serious?"

"Yeah. I don't hang out with those people."

The lights slowly began to dim.

"Who do you miss the most?" Gail asked out of the blue.

The question instantly changed the carefree mood. "I guess Evan. He was a cool guy."

"Oh yeah, you were friends, right?"

"We hung out sometimes."

"He was so great on the guitar."

"And he taught himself. He was a fucking genius." Marshall recalled the first time he heard Evan play. It was in Stuart LeSage's basement, and the half dozen kids in attendance were mesmerized. "Who do *you* miss?"

Gail took a moment to think. "Priscilla, I guess."

"It wasn't true about her being related to the Swanson TV dinner family, right?"

"Right," Gail said. "I have no idea who started that stupid rumor."

"I think it might've been *me*," Marshall confessed.

Gail chuckled. "Why do I believe that?"

The coming attractions were lame, but the movie was engrossing. Afterwards, Gail and Marshall strolled slowly in the brisk night air. The snow had stopped falling, and only bits of it were still on the ground, looking as if sections of the town had been salted by the sky. The clouds looked frosty. "What do you think of McKenna's theory?" Marshall asked.

Gail thought carefully before responding. "I don't buy it. Not a word."

"I'm glad you said that," Marshall told her. "I think there's some validity to it, but everyone's taking it way too seriously."

Gail hesitated, then blurted out the words that were on her mind. "Can I ask you a personal question?"

"Sure, but I'll tell you right now that I'm not gay, if that's what you were going to ask."

A warm grin lit up her face. "So how did you like the movie?" she inquired.

In the following morning's newspaper, a front page article stated that the police continued to gather evidence. It was determined that all the victims had been on some kind of antidepressant. There was only one psychiatrist in Solon Springs, but there were seven in Chippewa Falls and dozens in Madison. "Teen suicide is a major problem, not only in our community but in our country," Dr. Laurence Davenport of Chippewa Falls was quoted. "It's a very difficult, turbulent period of life. You must remind your growing children that suicide is not the answer."

Ten days after the double suicide, a group of six sets of distraught parents decided to be proactive. At eight PM, they drove to the lethal stretch of Highway 53 that narrowed into two lanes, and parked their vehicles on the shoulder of the road. With them were lawn chairs, flashlights, paperback books, blankets, radios, bottles of pop, cups of coffee, and turkey sandwiches on white bread. On the other side of the guard-rail, they spaced themselves out so that most of the quarter-mile of road was covered. They ate their sandwiches, read their paperbacks, listened to their radios, and waited. A few minutes after midnight, the Greyhound bus zoomed past them, travelling at the speed limit. Not one student was seen anywhere near this stretch of highway. When the big white bus had passed, the last set of parents, all twelve adults burst into wild applause. With pride dripping from their pores, they lifted their arms, danced to the music in their heads, and rejoiced. They were certain they had saved the life of a Solon Springs youngster.

But late Sunday morning, a bit of news made its way around the community like a fast-spreading virus. David O'Shaughnessy had jumped from the roof of the tallest building in town. Despite having been caught stealing small items from local stores and pieces of jewelry from the homes of neighbors, he was well-liked by his classmates.

How David got to the roof of the eight story office building was a mystery. One theory was that he hid in a bathroom on Friday night and spent the next day prowling around the floors. Another theory was that the security guard had been drinking on the job and neglected to lock the front door. To the people of Solon Springs, none of this mattered. Another teenager had ended his life.

There was something about David that Gail liked. He was a bit of a firecracker, threatening to explode at any moment, but underneath the brash exterior Gail saw a sweet young boy who just needed attention. His parents had been divorced for years, and his mother worked such long hours at the hospital that she was hardly ever home. "The rest of his life," she whispered to herself. "So much potential, despite what McKenna says."

Without analyzing, Gail grabbed a piece of typing paper and a pen, and began writing. "The dead students were all in McKenna's class. You might want to check that out." She didn't sign her name. She folded the sheet of paper and put it in an envelope addressed to the local police station.

It didn't take long for Mr. Theodore McKenna to be called into the station for questioning. McKenna, a graduate of Brown, had been teaching science and psychology for fifteen years. Divorced, he lived alone and was considered a personable, polite member of the community. Standing in front of a classroom, he had a charismatic, big brother appeal. Some of the female students wanted to sleep with him. Some of the male students wanted to play basketball with him. "I understand you dabble in hypnosis," Officer Herbert said.

"I don't dabble in it," McKenna responded. "I'm a licensed hypnotist and have cured people of smoking, drinking, and other unhealthy vices."

"Do you practice this on a regular basis?"

"Not in the past few years. Too busy teaching."

The police found no evidence that linked McKenna with any of the suicides. Still, every student in every one of McKenna's classes was called in.

"He taught science, mostly," Gail told Officer Herbert. "But he had a way of conveying his beliefs in the facts that he taught."

"I'm not sure what you mean by that," the officer said. "Religious beliefs?"

She hesitated. "No."

"Political beliefs?"

She hesitated. "No. Beliefs about life in general."

"Don't all teachers do that to some degree?"

"No," Gail stated. "They don't."

"Can you give me an example?"

Gail fidgeted in her chair. "He once told us that wherever we are in our lives right now, that's where we'll be when we're forty, fifty and sixty…that nothing will change…that we're already the people we'll be. If we're stars on campus, we'll be stars in life. If we're misfits and losers, we'll be misfits and losers in life." Gail waited for the officer to comment, but he was writing all this down. "Mr. McKenna has an odd way of looking at you. I mean literally. It's like he's hypnotizing you. I never look him in the eye. I think he's a little strange. But some of the other kids, a lot of them actually, look up to him like he's some kind of guru."

"Why do you think that?"

"Because they *need* some kind of guru, I guess."

"Do you think the students who killed themselves looked at him that way?" Tears suddenly exploded from Gail's eyes. She shook her head affirmatively, then buried her face in her hands. "I know this is hard," the officer said. "But it's very important. Did Mr. McKenna talk about the suicides with your class?"

"After every one, he asked us to take part in a moment of silence. But that's about it. Then he continued teaching like nothing happened, like it was just another day."

The following morning, the local newspaper reported that Mr. McKenna and every one of his students had been interrogated by the police. A major part of the story was that each student who committed suicide was in this teacher's class. All of a sudden, public opinion took on a ferocious life of its own, and McKenna was guilty before proven innocent. The community needed a scapegoat, and he was their man.

Parents forbade their children to attend McKenna's class. Still, some devoted students showed up and McKenna taught them as if nothing unusual was happening in the outside world. As each day passed, the residents of Solon Springs became more agitated. On the tenth day after the previous suicide, people prayed no one would die. Parents made sure their children were safely at home. Some parents stood guard all night. The rapid heartbeat of the town was almost palpable. Everyone waited with bated breath for morning to arrive, dreading any news that might be travelling through the community like a snowball gathering speed as it rolled downhill.

When Gail's cellphone rang at nine o'clock the next morning, she rushed to grab it. "Thank you for telling me," she said. Then she clicked off. Immediately, she dialed Marshall. "Did you hear?"

"No," he said.

"Another suicide."

"Fuck," he muttered. "Who?"

"You won't believe it," she said.

"Tell me."

"McKenna. He shot himself."

"That son of a bitch."

Expectedly, the news spread like fire on a gasoline leak. The entire town was stunned and buzzing. Parents of deceased children were up in arms, now knowing that McKenna must've been responsible for the suicides. "The guilt must have eaten him alive," one parent was heard saying at a community memorial service.

No one would be the same - not the parents who lost children, not the surviving students, not the colleagues of Theodore McKenna who wished they'd sensed something. After a few days, the tremendous initial shock diminished. As the weeks slowly passed, not one suicide was reported. The black cloud that was devouring Solon Springs had moved on.

Room 52
IMAN CAROL FEARS

Asylum

"Hello?" A female voice, rising above the thud of the waves.

"*Hello?*" There's something high and lucrative in the murmur of her voice. I squint at her through the white sunlight.

"Can you see me?" A girl in a thin white hospital gown is lying at the edge of the lake. The hungry tails of the water lap at her dirt-caked kneecaps.

I say nothing.

The s-like curves of her frame are drawn into a crucifix on the hot sand. I imagine briefly that her body is one gorgeous sandbag, and the stitching along her calves and feet and elbows will come undone and white sand will pour from her ragdoll body.

Her eyes shine like black molten glass.

She continues: "You can. It's just that most people can't."

This girl's skin is that universal copper of equatorial peoples, forests of Burma and Belize, water-weary steppes of Morocco and Timbuktu.

The white rim of her gown is tinged green with algae.

"Most people can't see you?"

"Well, no, not usually." Her voice is all sawdust. I can tell what she is. They're easy to spot. Girls who yawn from man to man, from corner to corner, stretching starlight between gaps of fishnet stockings—

"Oh? Why's that?"

"They just can't. But you can, so, um, thanks." She looks as if she were about to exit barefoot across the grass; instead, she leaps with scorpion-like delicacy towards my feet.

"I wanted to talk to you because I thought you might be a writer." The eyes widen in calculated anticipation.

"I'm not." I reply. "Well, kind of. I write research stuff for an agency."

"What sort of research?"

"Psychology."

"Technology?"

"No. Psychology."

"You have a degree."

"B.A."

"That's nice. I'm going to college in the fall, and I'm only sixteen," she says. "That's not a lie."

I emit a sort of helpless grunt of affirmation.

"I was hoping you'd be a writer," she's saying. As she speaks, her skin becomes thinner, almost transparent. It's as if I can see through her ribcage, watch her inhale and exhale heavily. Her pale bronze-scaled lungs struggle against the flimsy white material with the effort. "There's something very impractical about you."

"Oh."

The hospital gown is cut wrong, too loose on her. It makes her look like an empty canister.

"So earlier," she says, "when you had your head in your hands, were you praying or meditating or—I mean, people don't usually stay still that long."

"Maybe I was doing both."

She nods furtively. The large brown-black eyes grow even larger, threatening to swallow my face whole.

"When you asked if I could see you, I thought you might be an angel." I'm actually half-serious.

"But I *am* an angel," she says, smiling this sort of bloodless, thick-lipped smile that's at once intoxicating and disturbing. I can't stop looking at her mouth.

Her face flickers in and out of focus. Her lips seem covered in something, maybe pepper.

"That'd be timely."

"What are you sad about? Did a woman leave you?"

"It's more that I can't decide whether to leave her. My wife—"

"You have a wife? I'm sure she's very beautiful. What's her name?"

"Lydia. She was born in Italy—"

"Brunette?"

"No. She was born in Italy, but she's not Italian…she has blond hair and blue eyes."

"Oh. So what are you upset about?"

"She's with another guy, now."

"I'm sorry to hear that. Do you have any children with her?"

"One. A girl."

"How old?"

"Six."

"Aw," she sighs in the way that you're supposed to when someone talks about their kid. "Is your daughter's name Clara?"

She doesn't give me any time to continue, just says:

"We put on a play in first grade. We were studying Egypt, so it was a sort of Egyptian version of Cinderella, and the point of the play was that no one liked Cinderella because she had pale blondish hair and watery green eyes and skin like smooth papyrus. Which everyone in class knew was ridiculous because that's the only kind of beauty that really counts.

I was an ugly stepsister. I told myself that this was a good thing, that it would be a fantastic acting opportunity, but really I wanted to be Clara—a little blonde French girl who'd been chosen for the lead—with the yellow hair and watery eyes. I wanted to scrub my own features out until I was shapeless as red clay and then remold myself beautiful. Anyway, Clara...her name was Clara."

I have no idea how to respond to this, so I focus on the name: "Uh, you're close, but its name—her name—is Chloe..."

It feels weird to mention my kid out loud. I generally only think of it at mealtimes.

"I wish I was at war," she says, unprompted. She's inching closer to me on the wooden bench. And the lake is glinting silver under the white gaze of the late morning sun.

"I want to kill myself all of the time for no particular reason," she's saying, still smiling. "I think I'd be less irrational if I had real problems—if I were a soldier, or if I was a refugee, or a prostitute, even—" This comes in a rush of half-choked thought.

"I've thought about it, too," I agree, surprised by how calm my voice can sound when speaking to a crazy person. Talking to her is like discussing female circumcision over fruit tarts.

"You ever read any Socrates?" And I have to look up to make sure it's still her speaking, even though there's no one else around.

"Yes."

"Then you're lying. Socrates never wrote anything down.

How old are you?"

"Twenty-six."

"That's old. So you were born in…"

"1985."

I feel kind of old. Sometimes I think I'm already inching towards senility, but that's probably just the drugs. I look down and my hands are shaking.

She gets on her knees in the dirt by my feet.

"I'm sixteen," she murmurs. "I was born in 1994." And she smiles that thick bloodless smile until I return it. We're a couple of baboons.

"Sixteen. God, that sounds young," she whispers, letting her hand trace circles along the fabric of my thighs. "You seem nice, though. I hate that you're nice."

As an afterthought, she alleges: "I wish you were meaner so you would fuck me."

The whites of her eyes roll towards me with this sudden recklessness; her yellow fingernails rake at the soil. A green inchworm is ticking its way across the tops of her breasts.

I think for a moment we both believe that the conversation has smashed to pieces on the ground.

"You wish I were meaner so I would—what?" I say, even though I heard her.

"Never mind," she says. She stands and stretches, tossing her arms like dice at the sun-drenched water, at me.

A streak of dirt lays like a dash of black paint across her cheek.

"What's it like, being in love?" she hums, softly.

"Like you would do anything for that person. Like you would cease to exist if that person left you."

"Sounds like shit."

I laugh kind of noncommittally. And now I'm thinking about what it would be like to fuck this girl—

"The trouble with me—with our generation—" she's saying, in a tone of voice indicative of lighting a cigarette—she smelled faintly of smoke— "is that fame is our addiction, and documentation is our placebo. We're constantly diagnosing and re-diagnosing ourselves, with the help of over-worried parents.

"It's a crystalline stimulant called notoriety, available in a more condensed, crack like form than it was to any generation before us—so deceptively close that we can taste its odor with the skin of our eyelids. We're not the first generation to dismiss our parents' morality, but we're the first to grow up without even knowing what it is."

I nod. She's talking too much.

"What did I look like when I came out of the water? Was I like Aphrodite in that Botticelli painting?" She's still smiling, dragging her knees across the sand and dirt.

"A bit."

"Let's repeat the process." She stands and rushes to the shore, dunking herself under the surface of the water and then rising from it with hot radiance. "Excuse me, sir? Sir? Can you see me? Oh, thank you, thank you so much—most people can't."

I don't want to look at her and so I look up at the sky. Above us, prism-like clouds gather like cracked patches of stained glass at the whisper of her voice. My hands start to shake harder.

"Your hands are old," the girl comments, holding one of my hands up to the sun. It looks old, translucent, under the hot white light. "You think I'm insane," she repeats, grinning.

"I can't stay much longer. I have to be someplace soon. At noon." I'm not lying; I have to pay my dealer. And then I have a parent-teacher conference with my wife and six-year-old.

"I have an appointment with my psychiatrist at 11:30. In Como. No, in St Anthony."

There was a society I hadn't been admitted to in undergrad—Saint Anthony Hall, I remember. An order of blond aristocrats, lips dripping perpetually with gravy—

"Can you drive me to my psychiatrist's office?" she asks. Her thighs are still wet. "I'm not supposed to ride with strangers, but you seem, unfortunately, harmless."

"I am," I say. Mostly.

"Have you ever killed anyone?" Her manner is a little too reproachful, a bit too delicate.

"No. Thought about it...the man my wife was with."

"She was willing."

"I suppose."

"You're still in love with her."

"I am." I admit, staring at the girl harder. The sun is getting hotter and the wind starts to pick up.

I decide she's one of those girls who look pretty when they're young but don't age well. Her hollow adolescent beauty wasn't going to survive the harsh sunlight. She might be middle-aged in minutes.

"I'm on about five different psychoactive drugs right now," she's murmuring, making a daisy chain out of the wilted white wildflowers on the grass at our feet.

I'm on more than that, I want to say, but don't. Instead I tell her that: "I'm on about three myself."

"I have prom in a few days," she begins, in a tone that insinuates that she'd smiled, cordially, at my last remark, digested it, and decided it was shit.

I just nod. There's something lucrative and inconsistent in this girl's voice; the sound of it is intoxicating.

"My dress is white," she's saying with a bit of a whimper, stringing the wildflowers together with strands of nubile grass. "If you're still a virgin your senior year, you have to wear white. I hate being a virgin."

Let me fuck you, then, you crazy bitch, I want to tell her. But she's sixteen, so I just smile and say, "That's good, at your age."

"Not really. I just really want someone to have sex with me. I stopped caring who a long time ago."

This last confirms my theory about women:

Women are their own agents of destruction.

Their lives are like dry leaves doused in kerosene, and they're constantly craving a match.

"That's not good," I tell her.

"Will you?" Her voice travels with a beam of this almost visible green light to my ears. I can feel the drugs starting to kick in: the sun-drenched lake was writhing like a pool of green beetles behind her tiny body.

"Will I what?"

"Will you fuck me? I'm on a birth control stick, see, it's in my arm. Mom had it put there. Feel."

She extends a plump, golden arm with this sick, sort of saccharine grace, as if she expected me to stroke her. I don't touch it.

It's already relatively clear that this girl deals in subterfuges, that deception is her currency.

"You're too young," I say. "I'm married."

"Can I kiss you?" she asks. "I just want to kiss you once."

"Um, no."

"Why?"

"You're too young. But that's—sweet of you, I guess."

Sweet—I'd split her like a rotten cantaloupe.

Her phone rings. I notice that the sound is unmarked by her, neutral and inhuman, like the smooth sand at her feet. It's that metallic, songless tune every phone has before the consumer customizes it—or consumes it.

I play a game in my head with the words: customize, consume, costume, carnival, carnal, carnivore, carnivorous...

She picks it up. "Hi, Mom," she murmurs, stepping off to the side on brown ankles.

I wait a bit and the phone conversation is finished. "That's my mom. She's picking me up, soon."

"I should go," I falter. "I have to walk to my appointment."

"You can't," she pleads, and she's disarmingly sincere.

*

She puts her forehead to mine "Pretend I'm an angel again, so I can solve the problem of your wife and daughter."

Our faces are centimeters apart; I can see each of her irises like the black marble entrance to an outdoor seraglio, choked with indifference.

"Alright."

"First I need to know if you've ever attempted suicide," she says, and her tone is kind of flat, as if she discusses this too often. And I'm wondering where she hurts or even if she does when I look up at her and say, "Not seriously."

"Me, too. Not seriously. I'm incredibly spoiled. I don't have real problems, so I invent them. What's suicide? There's a song by my favorite band: The only difference between martyrdom and suicide is press coverage.'"

Press coverage...she doesn't need any, I decide, she's a walking broadcast, a billboard for the terminally fucked-up. Try to suppress her and she'll sink back into the water.

She's already lived too long—it was someone, maybe

Diderot, who said that women all die at fifteen.

I realize I haven't responded to her yet and say, "That's better than having real problems."

"I guess," she says, and I can feel her breath like salt against my neck. "I want to kill myself half the time; the other half of the time I think I'm going to be the greatest writer of the century. Your wife, then—you love her."

"Yes."

"Even though she made you angry."

"Yes."

She says nothing for a moment, then smiles widely. "Come play with me. We can fuck the pain away." She runs back to the muddy shore and splashes herself, drizzling water all over her clothes, dousing herself in it like kerosene. I just stare.

"I feel so dead," she's saying, and a few minutes have passed with me just watching the outline of her small, curvy body through the soaked white fabric of the hospital gown. "This is what I do when I feel dead." She lifted the edge of the fabric, running her right hand up one brown thigh.

"Please don't. It's probably just the drugs."

"You're right," she agreed, grudgingly. I watch her return back to shore and kneel in the sand.

"God, you suck," she whispers. The clouds grow thicker, as if the daylight has shattered at the rich inconsistency of her voice.

She's next to me on the bench once again; I don't remember seeing her walk up to it.

"I know."

"What's your name?"

"Adam."

"It's nice to meet you, Adam."

"What's your name?"

"I don't have one, I'm an angel." This remark is followed by a laugh that's both loose and callous, like the beating of bats' wings.

"Why did you ask if I could see you?"

She casts her eyes down. I know I'm tripping, now—her eyes are glinting like a fistful of wet olives. I can see houses of cards bobbing around her on the lake surface, made of human skin.

"I wanted to stop being real. Just for as long as it took you. I'm good at serving. And waiting."

The girl smiles again, sad and jaunty and drenched with light, then says, cheerily: "Soon, it'll be the longest day of the year. Did you ever watch for the longest day of the year and then miss it? I always watch for the longest day of the year and then miss it."

"That's from the Great Gatsby."

"And so are you."

She was either a brilliant actress or indeterminably insane. Her smile was wide; her teeth were bright and pristine as a cadaver's.

She spoke again while unhooking the top of her dress. "Your daughter. Has she seen you and your wife fight?"

"Yes."

"That could be traumatic for her."

"I know."

"I feel terrible for her. Don't stay together just because of her. Kids hate that. Better to split up so she doesn't have to witness the fighting."

"That's—I guess you're right."

"You're in love with your wife, even with everything she's done to you."

"Yes."

"You're capable of love," she says, pulling down the front of her dress so I can see the faded navy of her bra over small breasts. "But is she?"

"That's a very good question."

"See? I'm an angel. I'm brilliant," she says, grinning. "I'll be an Ivy Leaguer in a few months."

For a moment she doesn't say anything. Her face sort of swims and flickers across my line of vision—and then it's like the whole world is turning into melting wax.

The leaves begin to drip from their limbs, the waves turn to a thick, molten substance that threatens to burn me alive. And I try to stay calm and to tell myself it's just the drugs but my hands keep shaking and I want very badly to tell her to put her clothes back on.

"Don't do that," I command. "Get dressed."

She does what I tell her, and then:"I do have a name. It's Kara."

"Nice to meet you, Kara."

"If I could," says Kara, "I'd erase the 2000s from my

memory, just blot out those ten years and replace them with something lovely and blinding, like hot white cotton dipped in arsenic."

I nod and press her brown left leg into the sand, running over the pale stubble with my fingertips.

"I'm scared," Kara says to fill the silence, rotating her body on the thin layers of shifting sand. "I'm scared this has all been a dream, and when I wake up I'll be eight years old again."

I just nod.

"I'm six years old," she says with her eyes closed, sinking her right hand into my lap, "and I'm in that play, the Egyptian Cinderella. And I'd imagine that I was another girl, with shinier copper skin and two silk braids. The same boys who'd call me ugly would suddenly clamor to touch me, and I'd smile and let them slip their hands up my dress and I'd open my mouth wide for them like in the book. Because I'd rather be loved for something I can control than hated for something that I can't. And then I'd move on to other men, scores of them..."

"And they'd love you," I say, and already the universe was ending for Kara, the delicate pieces of her dream world were crashing about her ears.

"And they'd love me."

I trace the outline of her body through her hospital gown; her eyes close and she shivers visibly.

"I think about sex too much," she says.

She was re-hooking the gown; I watch the navy bra and the patches of wet brown skin disappear under the thin white fabric. "All of the time. Can't I kiss you? Please, just once—just touch me a little bit, I need it so badly—"

I can see her delicate face contorting with reckless biological desperation. Another woman throbbing for a match.

And it's the realization that I do whatever I want to her that makes her so repulsive. I can tear through her like a child ripping apart the pages of a coloring book. I can make her come and I can bring her close to death, leave her limp and gasping...

I can take my pocketknife and tear her mouth open at the seams.

I start to picture what that would look like, with all the blood and the world turning to wax around her corpse, and I tell her I think I should go.

I start to walk away from the girl and back up the path, where joggers march in endless circles about the lake..

"Did you hear what I just said?" she's screaming from the shore. "All I want is for you to hurt me."

I wish I can close her eyes and return her to the melting water. I'd bathe her in cataracts.

"Go see your psychiatrist."

"Don't go. If you go, I'll drown myself. Don't think I won't do it."

"I'm leaving now." I begin to walk more quickly, dodging yuppie parents with strollers and elderly couples in bicycling attire, all of whom are staring at me with bright, vacant eyes.

She follows me up the path like a snake.

"I won't leave you alone until you kiss me. Please." She's gripping my left hand with her tiny child's palm. "Just once."

I shuddered, loosening myself from her palm's insatiable grip. I watch my hand drip momentarily with thick wax.

Kara stares at me. Flecks of newspaper shreds—gossip columns, religious advertisements and green-washed obituaries—circle around her bare ankles. Shadows play at the edges of her eyes.

"I'll follow you," she murmurs. "Don't think I won't."

And I'm thinking about the thousands of things I can do to this girl, all of which begin with ripping off the gown and fucking her, hard, on the sidewalk before returning her to whatever institution she's just escaped from. And passersby are staring. I start to laugh.

The girl frowns. "Why are you laughing?"

She makes a pass for my lips but I turn my head; instead she kisses at my cheek.

"I hate you," she says. "I hope your daughter turns out like me."

"She probably will."

Chloe, and I'm thinking of my sleeping child in the nursery. *Chloe, Kara, Halie, Eurydice, Leiagore, Nausithoe, Orithyia, Lydia, Asia…*

Nymphets, all hung under gorgeous darkness, all straining under the weight of the sky—

"Adam?" She's several feet away, back on the shore—I don't remember her walking away. *Just the drugs.*

"What?"

"You should change her name. Your daughter's, I mean."

"To what?"

"Kara. Chloe's the worst."

"I'm leaving, now."

"If you go, I'll kill myself. I'm insane, I really am." Now her lungs are shining a hot transparent yellow; her mouth leaks kerosene.

I imagine tilting her head back a little harder, forcing myself into her mouth, just until she tastes the salt.

"You're an angel, right? Just go back to the water where you belong; you'll be fine."

Sirens, from far off.

Kara stands still in the water. She bites her lower lip. She's shuddering, the dark coiled mess of hair backlit, a sort of urine-drenched halo.

The girl had risen from the lake like Aphrodite in Botticelli's accidental masterpiece, splashed with carbolic acid and self-indulgent fantasy.

Kara's posture reminds me of my wife. Lydia. She bites her lower lip, too—she almost always smells of candied detergent.

My wife will toss blue glances at the child asleep in the next room, and then she'll push me against the bed and sink into my sternum...

And as the men in white unload themselves from their van, I hear a scuttling in the water, like a desperate aquatic bird flapping at the lake surface. And—I suppose this is when they loaded her back onto the stretcher—a scream; the sound of her voice tumbling listlessly amongst the waves.

I keep walking.

She's back in the ambulance. And a pair of concerned parents are probably stroking sweat from her forehead while she looks restlessly towards the hidden sky.

Room 64
CORTNEY DAVIS

Alchemy

The fourteen-year-old with dark eyes slouches on the exam table,
    says she wants to keep the pregnancy, that she understands
    how her life will change.

Her mother, who looks about thirty, sits straight in the chair and
    tells her daughter, you should terminate. The girl catches a
    breath. Does the mother remember what it was like before
    the first flutter, before the belly grew?

The mother cries, and we think she might strike her daughter. The
    daughter says, would you have terminated me? Then she
    becomes lean, slides off the table, becomes a wolf. She turns
    her thin nose to look at us.

None of us try to guess what will happen. We've seen so many
    transformations. The mother does love her daughter; the
    daughter loves her unborn child. At night, howling winds
    will keep them awake. They'll walk through snow too cold
    for any living thing.

Outside our closed door, the waiting room is crowded. Little girls
    and newborn babies, flowered headbands wrapped tight
    around their skulls.

Room 65
ROBERT LAUGHLIN

For the longest time, she tried to find its source

a house she'd lived in half her life should have no surprises
but now there was a ceaseless, muted sound she couldn't place
it never changed in pitch or volume
she heard it in every room
in time, it figured in the soundtrack of her dreams

she checked every utility and fixture
she had the house fumigated for calling insects
nothing helped

one day, the phone rang
she guessed who was calling
and knew there had never been any sound
what she thought she'd heard was the absence of sound
the sounds of human occupancy

widowed at twenty-two, she raised her brood alone
never was there a moment's stillness in the house
her son, now calling from his dorm, was the last to leave

she kept him on the line, greedy for his voice
finally hung up and wondered where she could get Muzak of
Keds treading sheet vinyl
Clarissa's explanations in the next room
dribbling in the driveway, heard through the outside wall
anything to dispel the clamoring quiet of the childless house

Room 66
ERIC VICTOR NEAGU

Jessica Dobson

When the Sheriff found Larry Laramont that August dawn, Larry was asleep against a tree, an old 0.22 rifle across his lap. Pink covered Larry's hands. In scattered spots that sprinkled his overalls the color had become darker, no longer neon bright. And the pink stained Larry's face where the camouflage make-up had rubbed off. Walking up to the boy, the Sheriff noticed Larry had grown tufts of sideburns that were sparse and weak. Then he spotted the minor pink explosion against the maple opposite Larry. He would comment in his report, a report he did not want to write, that it "took fifteen bullets before the nearsighted perpetrator destroyed the evidence." The Sheriff owned a poetic side, so had it not been official he might have written, "Not every first love is recalled fondly."

*

On low moraines and drained swamps they built the farms. Soon the fields of corn and soy undulated across vast expanses. Then they constructed the town. Wallaceville, Illinois. It rose out of a small valley cut by the creek. From those first days, the Laramonts had been residents. That was over one hundred and fifty years ago. The town never grew to more than five hundred residents. It was a stop along a westbound wagon trail then. When Larry forever changed the Laramont legacy, Wallaceville was barely holding at two hundred and fifty inhabitants. The Dobson family made it two hundred and fifty-three that summer.

In town, that handful of original families held rough but respected reputations. So Larry was given a healthy amount of legal latitude on more than one occasion, his school record being one such example. He was just ten and already the height of a man when his mother died. Over those next two years his attendance at school was sporadic. But because he was a Laramont, nobody said a thing. Later, at Pickem County Middle School, he discovered wrestling and his participation in class, though never outstanding, became more regular.

Larry had two reputations in high school. The first was for wrestling. As a freshman it was clear he was no random success. That year he narrowly defeated the previous state champion, a senior, at finals in Springfield. After that he became a town hero and his second reputation, for two *borrowed* cars, several large fights, and a small Fourth of July fire that threatened a neighbor's barn, was easy to forgive—boyhood shenanigans. When he met Jessica Dobson, two state titles later, he had already reached town legend status for wrestling and boyhood shenanigans, both. That was the summer before his senior year.

*

There were exactly four entrances into Wallaceville, each marked with elaborate antique signage carved out of limestone in the shape of covered wagons. Wagon wheels adorned either side of the signs. They were mounted to spin and when Larry needed to cut weight he ran from sign to sign. He would spin a wheel and run across town before the previous spin had stopped. Larry wanted to cut four pounds the day he first noticed Jessica Dobson. He only cut two.

"Who is that?" Larry asked. He stopped, forgetting his run entire, at a relative's house across the street.

Wilma Randolph, his mother's cousin by marriage, was observing and sipping sun tea with her neighbor, a three hundred pound near shut-in named Tamara. Wilma replied, "Them is my new neighbors, Datsuns or somethin'." Larry looked at Wilma; she explained, "Calls hisself Mayor. S'pose to run the new plant."

"Don't see how you could be a mayor if you ain't been a'lected. And you can't run a new plant until it's done bein' built," offered Tamara.

"The girl? Who is the girl?"

"Somebody got hisself a crush," Wilma playfully slapped Tamara. Tamara shook with laughter, "Hope she like wrestling." The women grinned.

Larry watched Jessica move. This girl, t-shirt clad, pegged jeans, soft leather sandals, long auburn hair, pale and beautiful, a girl unlike any he had seen. Jessica dropped a box on the way to the house. The Dobson dog stopped behind her, wagging its tail. Larry instinctively moved to help. The women laughed harder. He tried to put his hands in the pockets of pocket-less shorts.

"Go on, give her a hand Larry," said the fat woman.

Jessica picked up the box and went into the house. "They don't need no help," he mumbled.

The girl returned. From across the street he saw the dampened bangs, and he ogled her as Jessica lifted the front of her shirt from her breasts, allowing cool air in, dropping the shirt again, where it adhered to her chest. Tiny buds showed beneath the fabric, enough to noticeably excite a seventeen-year-old boy wearing loose shorts.

"Yep, that's a adequate girlfriend for young men," laughed Wilma.

The fat woman heaved uncontrollably, half-laugh, half-gasp for oxygen. "You need someplace to put that thing. I got plenty of space." Tamara waved hands up and down her ample physique.

Larry had exactly the place to put it, but it was at home behind the barn. Red in the face, he quickly ran there and fantasized about Jessica. All the lascivious excitement of youth dropped onto the grass in tiny beads and desire turned to satisfaction. But desire soon returned and Larry resolved to meet this girl. Somehow, in the middle of summer, they would have to meet.

*

Mayor, unhappily, would notice Larry long before Jessica ever did. Five weeks after moving to town, Mayor mentioned Larry to a local contractor working on the plant. Larry had just run by. It was 3:00. According to Mayor's estimation, it was the same time Larry had run along that stretch of highway for the past three weeks.

"Who is that boy?" asked Mayor.

"That's Larry's son," replied the man

"What's his name?"

"Larry."

"What's the boy's name, I mean?"

"Larry."

"What's your name?"

"Larry, but I'm no relation."

Mayor grimaced, "You know that boy runs by nearly every time my family steps outside of our house. We're in the front yard, he comes running up and down the sidewalk. If we're in the backyard, he comes up the alleyway."

"So, ain't a crime to jog. Besides he's conditioning."

"For what can a boy run all day long?"

"Wrestling. You seen his name. It's on damn near every sign into town."

The two men turned and looked at the wagon sign on the adjacent highway. Among other things, it read:

State Champions: 2003, 2004, 2005
Wrestling Larry Laramont.

*

That night Mayor picked Jessica up from her new friend's house. The friend lived in the country on a lonely gravel drive. Mayor hated these "country bumpkin" roads. One of the perks of his job was a new car. At any speed, the small rocks dinged and dented the car, depreciating the value of the perk with each pockmark. So when Mayor and Jessica slid into the driveway, he was already in a foul mood.

That was just after 6:00. Jessica, Larry knew, should have been home by 3:30, 4:00 at the latest. This 6:00 business disoriented him. All of his reconnaissance could be void if her schedule became erratic. If he could not rely on her to return from practice at a consistent hour, how could she be relied on for anything else? What if something was going on behind his back?

Jessica's absence radically altered Larry's routine that day.

Since the moment he laid eyes on her, his days had been structured around Jessica's comings and goings. The peak Jessica hours were between 3:30 and 5:00. It was then that she was home alone. It was then that Jessica would slip out of her loose track clothing and into a bikini, sunbathing in the afternoons, or into cutoff jeans and a tank top, reading a book on the porch. It was then that Larry would fill his mind with fantasies.

The fantasies took two forms. The first were often ethical, even romantic, in nature. But Larry found them impractical and unlikely.

Running by, Jessica drops something, perhaps a moving box, perhaps a grocery bag, but most often a small child. Oh no! The child stops breathing, for it was sucking on a piece of candy and the candy has become lodged in its throat.

Jessica, in a screamless panic, seeks help. Here comes Larry, just running, cutting weight, nothing more. Larry takes the position learned via video in health class. The child, writhing for breath, responds to the deft and strong hands, as Larry boldly performs the Heimlich maneuver to success. Phone numbers are exchanged. Week's end, Jessica and Larry, boyfriend and girlfriend.

Larry reserved the second fantasy for regular, often daily, visits behind the barn. These provoked guilt, so he controlled them as much as he could, out of respect for Jessica.

On a typical night, Larry's run would have ended with dinner, between 4:30 and 5:00, at Wilma's house. Because Jessica was not yet home, that evening he only planned to pause briefly at Wilma's to say he would be running longer.

"Instead of running yourself skinny, why ain't you just go and talk to the girl?" Wilma said.

"What girl?"

"That pretty one you leaving me for," goofed Tamara.

"You in love, boy. A'mit it."

He tried to change the subject. "I got another scholarship offer the other day."

"No time to study when you spend it all studyin' that little girl right there," Wilma nodded toward the Dobson's. Larry looked up. They were home. She was home. Mayor was there. Jessica was there. He stared. Long legs. Loose track shorts.

The women laughed, "You in love, boy. A'mit it."

Frustrated, bold, exhausted Larry walked across the street. The run had begun at 2:50 and did not end until that minute. Without realizing it, on the hottest day of the year Larry had run 21 miles, his longest ever, and all of it through a town that was less than half a mile wide. Mayor walked into the house. Jessica rummaged through the car for something lost. Larry stood outside of the Dobson fence, determined to discuss her sudden inconsistency. He had lost ten pounds of fluid during his extended run. Jessica bent further into the car. A behind the barn fantasy intermingled with fury at her tardiness. Then, without notice, the air left the world. Larry fell to the ground.

On a strange bed in a strange house he woke up. It was not much after 7:00. A dim light on in the room. This was a girl's room with posters of clean-shaven men Larry did not recognize. He

70

noticed a scent, and then another. A potpourri of perfumed items, shampoos, candles, fragrances he had never smelled before.

A school picture of Jessica on the nightstand. Senses returned. Larry touched the picture for reference, and then stuffed it beneath his shirt. Footsteps. Mayor entered the room. Jessica stood behind him, twirling her hair, never looking at Larry directly.

"You okay boy?" asked Mayor without concern.

"What happened?"

"I'd say your obsession got the better of you."

"I got to go."

"No son. You got to feel better first and then we got to talk."

Larry tried to sit up, "Sir?"

"You're going to promise me you won't run by this house again."

Instinctive sarcasm, "Not much town to run in." He sat up a little more.

"Jessica is a good kid. We don't need muscled-up stalkers bothering her, understood?"

The disorientation that had clouded Larry's mind lifted. He had not considered two things. First, he recognized that stern-faced Mayor did not like him. This made no sense. Every father of every daughter in town would gladly call Larry son-in-law if given the chance. And second, Larry acknowledged that the fall, the heat, and the heavenly scent of a young woman's room had conspired to loosen his bladder. Larry had wet himself in Jessica's bed.

Escape.

Mayor continued, "I just can't have boys, athlete or no, obsessing over my little one."

Escape with the evidence.

"I know it's nothing illegal, but I just don't think it's right, a boy obsessing after a girl that way."

In one motion, Larry lifts the sheets and comforter from the bed, hops to the floor, and bolts out of the room. Down the stairs, nobody notices the wetness. Out of the house, nobody follows. All are stunned. Nobody follows. At home, two washings later, Larry would sleep with the evidence for all of the coming school year, confident Jessica never suspected a thing.

*

School started and Larry was king again. His name adorned school walls when wrestling season rolled around. The only seeming hitch to his season was a dramatic drop in weight class that concerned the coach, but not Larry. Although they never spoke, Larry secretly dedicated every match to Jessica. With pen ink and a small knife, he tattooed a "J" on the inside of his right biceps, convinced it would give him added strength. He would watch the "J" flex when he went behind the barn. Larry was king.

State came and went and Larry was victorious at the lower weight class. Four state championships meant a scholarship to pretty much anywhere he wanted. During and after the season he traveled from college to college on recruiting trips; everyone wanted him. He entertained many of them, knowing all along he would go wherever Jessica went. Twice on these trips he was offered sex, then he thought of Jessica's likely disappointment and politely declined. By February he discovered Jessica's post-graduation plans and made arrangements for a scholarship at the same college. Surprising her with the news would have to come at just the right moment.

By the time the Sheriff found Larry in the park, Jessica had already lived in Wallaceville for a year. Larry never exchanged one direct word with her during that year. Larry could have asked her to any number of events. He had been given a rust-colored Firebird with a big block engine. She would have liked riding to prom in that, but she never attended any dances. Or he might have invited her to the senior parties that streamed through the summer after graduation. Those were weekend events. On the weekends, Jessica was never around. So Larry patiently suffered, confident that college would finally bring them together.

Then in August she appeared, magical, full of charm, a strange last effort at assimilation into a community she would soon leave. Larry noticed her immediately.

Ten, twenty-five, and then fifty students at the party. The field of corn grew in high stalks and surrounded three sides of the group. Cars parked haphazardly on the weak patch of lawn. A row of trees marked a nearby low area, where wetlands never converted to farm. At the edge of the field a fire pit, bonfire blazing in the sweaty air. Everyone of note was there, even a favorite teacher stopped over.

Larry was still the king, although his reign was waning. He absorbed large doses of bourbon from a bottle and spat it into the fire. Flames burst horizontally and the alcohol burned out on the opposite grass. He stopped spitting and drinking when Jessica walked out of the dark and into the firelight.

They were two then by the fire, the others had gathered around a truck bed where large speakers played and everyone cheered and danced. Larry full of drunken charm. Jessica cautious, yet graceful.

"You the new girl, right?" asked Larry, staring at the fire like some gypsy about to read a fortune.

Everything she said sounded like a nervous question. "Yes?" she replied with a smile. He was getting somewhere. She spoke again, "You were at my house last year? When you passed out from running too much?"

Alcoholic logic provoked confidence, "Maybe I passed out because of you." It came out wrong. Things became tense. She looked toward the group.

"I mean, because you're so pretty. No other girls around here like you."

"Thanks?" She smiled. Fire high now, higher than before. Larry offers a drink, she sips from the bottle. Then a statement, her first. "I feel like I don't know anybody here."

"Tough to move afore your senior year. When you come back next summer you should come to more of these little soirees."

Then the crushing blow that triggered the tirade. "Oh, my boyfriend and I are planning on getting an apartment together after this first year. He wants to go straight through the summers. My dad won't let us get married until we're done with school."

Larry never heard a word after "boyfriend." He looked out at the cornfields in inebriated sorrow. At that moment Jessica died to him. After several awkward seconds of bitter silence, she crept into the dark and away from Larry. When he looked up she was gone. Steady pulls from the bottle did not help. She was gone. Due to some random, unforeseen folly, she was gone. The fabric of the future had been rent.

Before the rampage, Larry spoke, briefly, to one last person. Ryan McCormick, a little guy who wrestled five weight-classes beneath Larry, stepped to the fire. Pale yellow firelight on their faces. Shit-faced and simple, Ryan bellowed, "You gonna horde that or share?"

Larry handed him the bottle, almost empty. "I might just quit wrestling."

Ryan reacted, "What the hell you goin' do that for? You a machine, a Warrior machine."

The bottle in Larry's hands now, "You still got that old deuce-deuce up in your car."

"Betty? Locked and loaded. Never know when a squirrel might need a nut. Plus, my mom won't let me have no guns in the house."

Out of the trunk Ryan withdrew a 0.22-caliber rifle, purchased at a yard sale. The box of shells was stolen. Drunken Larry pointed the gun at the moon, "Is she true?"

"Truer 'n shit," said Ryan, closing the trunk door on his Ford Escort.

"I be the judge and jury of that." Larry pointed the gun at the fire. They were 100 yards out. He aimed at a small hole through the wall of people and fired. Sparks flew out of the bonfire. People yelled. Larry smiled sadly. A young man scorned has little legitimacy.

*

Larry takes the gun and the shells and throws them into the tight backseat of his Camaro, Warrior singlet and headgear from State still there. No rules against drunken driving exist and nobody cares when he pulls away from the group and drives, headlights off. He knows Jessica has left. Given a car for graduation, a VW convertible, red. It is nowhere to be seen. He will find her and attend to the situation.

The pink spray paint he borrows from his father's shed. Meant to mark pavement, it will do. The green, black, and brown face paint are from Halloweens long past. He covers his face in camouflage, splotchy, without pattern. He fashions a shoulder strap out of dark leather belts for Sunday outfits and wraps the gun around his shoulder. He is ready.

Nobody can stop him, because he runs. He leaves his house, gun across back, carrying a bag; contents include eight cans fluorescent pink spray paint, one pint Early Times, one Nalgene bottle of water for dehydration. By Mayor's plant, nearly complete now, he runs, laying low in a ditch as a car passes. It is late, later than 3 A.M. Jessica is a girl, he reasons; girls have curfews. He runs by the wagon train sign and spins the wheel. This will be fast and fierce he tells himself.

From a tree in Wilma's yard he can see into the Dobson's home, into Jessica's bedroom. He loads and aims the gun at windows. Mayor, boom. Mrs. Mayor, boom. Dog, boom. Jessica, boom. He does not fire. Instead, he climbs down and snakes across the road in zigzag pattern, leaping and rolling commando style, stopping next to Jessica's car. The spray paint comes out. He paints. On either side and on the hood he paints, pausing at regular intervals, pink spray bleeding into pink spray, splotching his clothes. And then he finishes his task.

Retreat, not for fear, but for space. No good angle to get all four. Ducking behind a garden retaining wall, he fires twice. Air blows out of Jessica's right side tires. Nothing stirs and he leaps a picket fence, landing one foot in dog excrement. He ignores the foot and fires again, six times. More air escapes from more tires and the driver's side windows crumble. The boy wipes perspiration from his face. Camouflage comes off on his hand. He is not done.

This act is private, maybe just the family will know. Maybe Mayor will wake up early, find the car—nobody has stirred yet in the house—and fix everything. There must be more. Something grand must come. He waits and thinks.

He climbs Wilma's maple again. Eight shots in a town with two hundred fifty-three people. Somebody must have heard. The bourbon burns his dry mouth. Twenty minutes pass and the bourbon is nearly gone. No movement anywhere. He is in the clear. He no longer waits.

The idea. One last thing; a public record of this tragedy is needed, something Mayor cannot hide. For the first time he thinks of the family name, Laramont. It means something to him now. A one hundred fifty year reputation must be kept intact; a transient teenage girl cannot destroy a legacy. He must destroy the girl. There is only one way. The people must know a Laramont has been cuckolded.

The boy crisscrosses town. Running through the humid

night wall, drunken tears streak the camouflage. Footsteps pound the pavement. He does not hide any longer. He stops four times, exhausting six of the spray paint cans. And now there are four monuments, a broadcast to the world of Jessica's evil. His will be done.

*

The Sheriff was the first to notice Larry's monuments, though he was called to town for a different reason. Someone had heard multiple gunshots at the park: a picnic table with shelter, a cracked asphalt basketball court, and a swing set. Probably just kids, but Wallaceville had never had a problem of this nature in his two years at the county level. It was worth a look.

Larry would have been crushed by the Sheriff's passive reaction at his work. The planned statement of shock and awe so powerful to a drunken boy, registered only, "Hmm," from the Sheriff. And, "These folks ain't gonna like that much."

He drove into town and found the boy against a dying pin oak. He surveyed the scene and noticed the pink explosions against the maple bark twenty yards off. Streaks marked the boy's face and the Sheriff could see there had been some serious sorrow that night. The entrance to town was a likely testament to that sorrow.

"Upsy-daisy, son," he poked Larry with a baton. "Let's get you home. You got some cleanin' up to do." The boy grunted and stood with the Sheriff's help.

At the Laramont's, the Sheriff offered near condolences, "Looks like this one got hisself a broken heart."

Larry Senior replied, "Well, we all been there."

"It's the truth. That's a lesson we, all of us, endure."

*

At 5 A.M., about the time the Sheriff drove into town, Mayor Dobson woke and prepared for work. Two pieces of toast and a cup of coffee later, he walked to the garage and pulled his S.U.V. into the alley. The late summer light was dim on the horizon. He noted nothing unusual until he reached the drive into the construction site. Two cars, one a Mercedes, the other a BMW, already there. A meeting. Chicago investors. He had forgotten. Exactly fifteen minutes to run home and change clothes before several other high-end foreign cars would appear. He turned around in a hurry.

Three hundred yards toward home, the sun cresting the horizon behind him, exposing the world before him, Mayor slammed on his brakes. Anti-lock. They pumped to a halt along the gravel shoulder. There could be no doubt. Two hundred fifty-three people, only one Jessica Dobson. He read every word on the wagon wheel entrance to himself:

Welcome to Wallaceville, Illinois
Population: 250
Home of Wagon Train Dayz
State Champions: 2003, 2004, 2005
Wrestling: Larry Laramont
State Semi-Finalists: 1987
Girls Cross-Country: Stacy Johnston

And across the etched "Welcome to Wallaceville, Illinois," defacing, obvious, covering three feet of the eight-foot by ten-foot sign, Mayor read the pink bleeding spray painted sentence:

JESSICA DOBSON IS A WHORE

Room 78
JASMINE SWANEY

Snickerdoodle

My name is Victor Ripple and I am 60 years old. Don't ask me how I got your address; I literally had to pay $37 dollars for the privilege and now I'm a little worried that I have perhaps wasted my money.

You see, in 1957, I took the time to write Santa Claus a lengthy request for a Hula Hoop but instead he brought me a Slinky, which my drunken father subsequently unraveled and used as a wire to bind my mother's wrists. Then he emptied an entire rack of cooling blueberry muffins into a paper sack and sped off in our Nash Rambler. We never saw him again. Needless to say, I stopped writing to Santa.

I am not trying to imply that you are of the same ilk as Santa Claus. You are...cousins? In my mind, you all look like cartoon characters, especially Jesus. I guess what I'm trying to say is that I am going to give you the benefit of the doubt and assume that you have some sort of supernatural ability that might help solve a current and pressing problem of mine.

The problem goes like this: I had a passionate love for mediocrity and for my wife's Snickerdoodle cookies. I've never been a big dreamer; I'm the kind of guy who gets excited when he finds a dirty dime. So imagine my surprise when I was told by my wife that this wasn't good enough after more than thirty-five years. I first met her sometime between my insignificant existence at a subpar accounting school and my similar insignificant existence at a subpar accounting firm. At the time, she was gentle and cherubic. She called me "safe" and we got married. I was greatly relieved to find someone who could embrace my timidity. The years went by. Until one day I woke up and my wife was skinny and severe, and my whole head was bald. My wife left me for the man who put in our Anderson Windows. It was hard for me to watch him install those lovely double-paned glass panels without wanting to run to him, weeping liking a child. Could he not, for godsake, be quite so handsome? My pink flabby fingers were crushed in his handshake. As they tore out of the driveway - not in a Nash Rambler, but in my own sleek sedan - my wife threw out the car window, "You want to know the real problem? You could never make a decision."

Two days later, one of my back molars fell out. Five days later, and an incisor fell out. I have lost all my teeth; they simply leaped out of my head. I lost one chewing toast. I lost one on my walk to the office. It fell out of my mandible and straight into my shirt pocket, which was fortunate, like finding those dirty dimes. It's been exactly six months and four days since my wife took off and I am wearing a pair of dentures and staring at all 28 of my permanent teeth as they rest inside a glass jar on my desk.

Last night, I had a dream. In the dream, I saw myself with gargantuan hands. They were the size of my lost, sleek sedan. As the dream unfolded, I began uprooting whole trees. It was as easy as uprooting carrots with those hands. I awoke from the dream and very much wanted to use my hands in new and constructive ways. The first way I wanted to use them was as weapons to strike the face of the Anderson Windows Man. This I did in a parking lot as he and my wife were leaving an AA meeting together. He looked amused and she was clearly high on some sort of illicit substance or just pure hatred at the sight of me. I hit him square in the teeth and one lodged in my skin near a knuckle (there are actually 29 teeth in the jar; I kept his). I'll call anyone a liar who tries to claim that he felt the lion's share of the pain. My wrist hurts like an incredible bitch and a dollop of salve sits in the little pothole where his tooth so savagely punctured me. I'm sure I yelped when I hit him. My wife did a sort of dance on the spot while he rolled around. She looked so smug and delirious in her green pants suit. It made me wonder what kind of dreams the Anderson Man had beyond window installments. My parting words to her were in the shape of a question. "How was that for a decision?"

The second way I wanted to use my hands was as tools to write you this letter. Although I feel almost giddy after slugging someone in the face, I am pretty sure they are going to show up very soon and press some sort of charges. The charge I most fear is the one that will shoot up my spine if Mr. Window decides to smash my face into our marble countertops. I had a little surge of adrenaline in the parking lot, sure, but I am no warrior. I breathe heavily when I bend to tie my shoes; a bout of sustained violence will surely kill me.

So I guess what I am proposing is this: I am going to end

this letter and then tip all 29 teeth under my pillow before lying down for a short nap. You will appear from wherever you inhabit, wearing whatever it is you wear (I see you wearing a short, pleated skirt). As I sleep, you will use your wand to prop open my jaw before carefully yet efficiently (they could arrive any minute) placing all 28 of my teeth back into my head where they once belonged. The 29th tooth – the Anderson Man tooth – you will keep for yourself at a price of one million US dollars plus one old, dirty dime. (Put the million in a briefcase by the bed and the dime under my pillow.) You will also replace every single hair I ever lost back onto my head and return them all to the color they so vibrantly exhibited when I was twenty-three years old. Additionally, you will restore my bodily appearance to that of its twenty-third year but allow me to retain every bit of knowledge that now resides inside my brain after 60 years. Next, you will fly down to our kitchen and place the entire batch of cooling Snickerdoodles into a paper sack and set it next to the briefcase. Finally, watch over me – feel free to do a little naughty dance in that pleated skirt – until you hear my sleek sedan pull into the driveway. Then, rouse me with a kiss and I will courageously breeze down the stairs and meet them in the foyer. So stunned will they be by my youthful appearance that they will neither move nor say a word. With the sack of cookies and briefcase in one hand, and a dirty dime in the other, I shall spin on my heels and flip the ten cents to my wife. "Some hot dish in a pleated skirt just gave me this," I will say in a voice similar to John Wayne's. "Oh, and by the way," I will add, "I made these Snickerdoodles myself. Any asshole could do it." Then I'll climb into that sleek sedan and ride it downtown and out into the countryside until I die from exuberance. I'm looking forward to your utmost cooperation, and to a lifetime full of hindsight encased inside the skin of a young man.

Sincerely,

Victor Ripple

Room 81
H.V. WHITEHEAD

Exit Bag

You won't find me in the Yellow Pages. My website is under permanent construction. My Facebook page states that I work in customer services, which, all things considered, is not an untruth. My Twitter status still says, 'So this is Twitter.' I am the antithesis of an obstetrician. My repeat business is nil. My projected future business is infinite. My clients think I am their saviour, but I never hear from them again. If I do, I've failed. Or they have. Even then, they always come back.

Visit www.amazon.com and type in 'helium tanks.' Look at the 'Customers who bought this item also bought' section and you will see, amongst the balloons and bubble machines, book titles such as 'Break the Bipolar Cycle,' 'Why Am I Still Depressed,' 'Final Exit,' 'The Best Way to Say Goodbye,' 'The Peaceful Pill Handbook,' and 'Obsessive Love.' You will also find adult oxygen masks, and for reasons of which I am oblivious, a 'no more mildew' shower curtain. This is not a fabrication. Feel free to investigate for yourselves.

My office walls are adorned with postcards from all over the world: the Empire State Building, the Grand Canyon, Mount Fuji, the Golden Gate Bridge, the Aurora Bridge and of course Zurich. I have quite the collection of postcards from there.

People find me when there's nowhere else to go. I don't advertise, but I'm not hard to locate. Forums, chat rooms, help groups. I make sure I'm present everywhere I might be needed. I'm a lot like God--when people get really desperate, they go looking for me.

My agency is full service. I book flights, always return: hotels, tours, dinners, skydiving, escorts, whatever you want. I use my client's credit cards for everything and those cards, they get well used. It's logical, if not fully ethical; if you're not going to be present when the bill arrives, are you really concerned as to your outstanding balance? My fee is paid in cash or over PayPal; payment has to be made at least one month before the event.

I'm sure you're speculating as to where my value really lies, after all anyone can book a hotel. Dear friend, I must impress upon you that this is the most important vacation you could ever schedule and you want to ensure all the details are perfect. That's where my real expertise becomes invaluable. I will tell you the mortality rate from hanging is 80% and I will explain that death normally occurs in five to seven minutes. With jumping, I will tell you that if you want to be certain, you need to jump from at least 150ft over land and no less than 250ft over water. I will send you the instructions on how to make an exit bag and I will have the helium tank delivered to your home along with balloons. The balloons are just for show.

Are you disgusted? I find that a strange reaction as I'm unremittingly proud of what I do. I grant people their final wish. I give people the choice that we forget we have. More importantly, I get to play God every single day. My e-mail box is always full. I sleep well at night. I'm here if you need me.

Room 83
DENNIS MAHAGIN

Abduction

Ed Munch
of Massapequa,
suffering much
with fibroids in the solar
plexus, slick half moon
cysts and then some,
with bald head thrust
between knees

on the floor
of the sick room—
Ballard Hospice, bars
on stained glass—Edward
with jowls the color of sunflowers,
advances upon end-stage liver failure,
tossing his lunch on the tiles, Ed begs,
between shallow frothy rasp, heave
and retch, for egress, for egress.

Only a year ago, he'd been stocking shelves
at a Pensacola gallery when the illness bloomed,
a scab on his wrist, which he picked, and rubbed,
like a scratch-off lottery ticket, he bled

in streaks, like Pollock upon
the polished cover of a Nolde print,
he swooned, and stumbled
from the curator's room, a dozen
slack jawed stares in his wake.

Only a month ago,
they'd been pumping him
with Dilaudid at night,
to adjust his palette for what was

coming, in the soft lamp light he
watched his long fingers sprout pink
caterpillar fuzz, knuckles morphed
into hinges for Monarch butterflies,
and Edward laughed, thinking to
simply shake his bone erosion
and jaundice like a common cold.

Today they've taken
the opiates away, inexplicably
in favor of time-released Interferon
with no magical properties, better
for the injured spleen
while squeaky-toed nurses come
and go in loose white shifts,
with pursed lips and a practiced
judgment behind professional
eyes, they've come to watch
Edward die.

"Are you alright, Mr. Munch?" one
of them inquires; she stacks the bedpan
brimming with cocoa-colored stool atop
an untouched cafeteria tray, she lets the plates
clatter with a lackluster hate, simply because
she can, "Can you stand?" she asks
coldly, "we really need to get you
back in the bed."

"I was a painter," Edward says,
hours later, to the quiet night, quaking
then, at the sudden sight of a pint-sized
extra-terrestrial intruder with almond
tear ducts and celestial breath-plumes
arcing like comet tails through the pool
of moonlight in his tiny room;
the creature nods
appreciatively at a charcoal landscape
etching Munch had made in a moment

of lucidity, one afternoon last month,
or was it the month before?

"I saw you, Munch whispers,
"on the bridge, the vanishing point,
the most innocent eyes ever in the
universe. And I wonder… is it done?
You know I've already begun a series
in copal, called Star Spatter Deep
Space, and I am so very ready
to be gone from this place…
Any time, really, any
time you are."

Room 86
GEOFF KAGAN TRENCHARD

27th and San Pablo

The Quarter-Pound Giant Burger across the street from my
apartment is a greasy beacon of light that watches the liquor store
close and the crack den open. This is where the still but furious grill
is the only thing that covers the smell of half-spilled beers and piss,
of stale cigarette roaches and used-condom slugs clogging the
gutters.

Perched alone inside at the counter, there is a woman,
mini-skirt squeezing her chicken-skin thighs like cellophane.
Vinyl tube top presses her breasts so hard against her chest it cuts
her cleavage like a loaf of bread. This is where you hope people
aren't what they look like. The lone cook on duty is a leathery prune
in a stained apron with wrinkles under his eyes that claw down to
his jaw. Out of the alley struts a Mack truck in a do-rag. Thick neck
of a forty-ounce fit snug in his left hand. A stride with the kind of
fury that makes my fists ball in my pockets.

He runs right next to me at the take-out window and shouts, *THE
FUCK YOU SITTIN' DOWN FOR?*
She snaps, *I'm taking a break, Martin.*
Well you restin on my investment, bitch.

Well, maybe you need to quit making so many deposits… bitch.
He cracks knuckles wrapped in platinum. They pop hollow in the
cold air. You have to wonder what it's like to come home to a
backhanded hello. To get into a fight that starts because you didn't
order dinner to go, and ends with a re-opened cigar burn on your
shoulder. For a second, she looks at me like her boat's sinking and
I'm just standing on the dock.

Then, *THE FUCK YOU STARING AT?* is shouted in my ear so
loud, I feel it more than hear it. This is where a woman was found
face-down under an overpass the other night, a black plastic bag
from the corner store knotted around her neck in a wrinkled scarf. I

imagine a blade cold as a railroad track sliding under my chin. A
motel mattress rushing up to my face as it soaks my blood down to
the box-spring. Swallowing the knot in my throat I say, *Nothing.*

Martin punches a window like it owed him money.
But now he's gone and got the cook involved. There is a steady
hand moving under the counter and the clap of metal gears
as a round advances to the chamber.

This is where loud cracks in the middle of the night never mean
a car backfiring. Where the tension pulses in time with the neon
sign. Martin makes it my lucky night and backs down the alley.
Arms up in a vulnerable goal post, bottle dangling in his grip like an
empty windsock, face fixed to a high beam glare of *Imo see you, later.*
This is where I cross the street to a warm, dry port.
Count my change, loose blessings, and feel her gaze
follow me from the corner as the deadbolt slides home.

Room 88
PATRICK WITHERELL

Someone Deserving

It is what it is. Thirteen bodies slumped in hushed unison. All joined in an unconscious gathering, a circle of sorts. Piled beneath tables and under chairs. Wherever they chose to take cover. Ring around the rose-colored pool of blood spilling into the middle of the room. There's nothing much to say except this isn't how it was supposed to happen. Not this way.

* * *

"What do you want to be?" They asked you in preschool, when you filed in with mom's fresh peanut butter and jelly sandwich, backpack strapped with confidence and vigor. You answered: a superhero, a pro athlete, the President of the United States. In elementary school: a race car driver, maybe a musician, an actor. What is it you want to do with your life? In middle school you wanted to be a teacher, a computer game designer, an architect. What will you be able to tolerate doing every day for the rest of your life? Explain why you are willing to do this until you die, until your last days on this earth.

When you are in high school they asked you again. Choose what you want to do. Pick your future. This is a multiple choice test, just so you know; we don't really have limitless options. Just fill in the corresponding box and flow down the path of least resistance. It's easy to think: what gives me the most options? Where can I make the most money? It's easy to ask the questions now, out of fear more than anything else. You don't want to end up like those people on the side of the street begging for stray condiments to suck down their dry throat. You want structure, security. By now you're not stupid, you aren't innocent. You want whatever means a three car garage. Three cars to be housed in that garage. The house too, white picket fence, some little kids running around. You want to know how to get your grubby hands on all of this.

When you're finished asking questions, finished figuring out what it is you will contribute to society, they ask you; well what are you willing to sacrifice? An off-hand question when you're finally making your precious twenty five dollars an hour. Can you come in on Sunday? We can't afford giving you a bonus this year. It is what it is, just so you aren't surprised. This is the world we live in. Just when you think you've made it, you realize everything was a house of cards toppling down on top of you. Now they ask you, do you get it? Can we count on you to do this without expecting anything more? Are you willing to remain static in your responsibilities to this company? If you want to keep your job, just nod your head. They thank you for your kind cooperation. While you walked out the door, they asked if they can count on you again, you know, to just sit there and take it. We're taking liberties in translation here, but you get the point.

Fast forward sixteen years with a massive headache you can't seem to get rid of, metaphorically speaking. The ringing and ringing in your ears: copy machines churning, computers buzzing, constant yapping of nothing important. You just want silence now.

Finally, silence is near, the light at the end of the tunnel. But somehow, silence seems like it is going to be loud as fuck. They ask you to come into their office. They speak in measured rhythm and tactical dialogue. Straightening their ties and dusting their suits while explaining the reality of termination. They want new, fresh, young. This isn't multiple choice were talking about here. There's one answer. And if the answer isn't you, it's somebody else. It is what it is, those are their exact words. Times, they are changing. It's not you, it's us. Repeat all bogus one liners for breakups. Over and over. And you knew it was coming, but still, this leaves a void.

To fill the void: crossword puzzles, daytime soap operas, pottery, sculptures. It is what it is.

If you could leap ahead in time and see the result of what filling the void without emptying the anger and aggression results in, this is it. If you could see the bodies resting in peace at the center of the room, you'd question their validity. Snarled in a suspended stockpile. Hands over feet. Feet over heads. Heads over unrecognizable body-parts. Unrecognizable body parts over cups of ice cream left unfinished, melting on the table. Pistachio, cookies and cream, chocolate, all dripping their milky residue where they stand. Think about that annoyance when there's ice cream dripping on your hands and you can't rinse it off. That's called a bummer.

Now, imagine that running lactose delicacy blended with chunks of human flesh, sprinkles of skull, and dollops of the finest hemoglobin. That's called a really shitty day. That's the kind of stuff you don't get over without an army of psychiatrists and a whole damn fleet of Prozac.

Still scanning the scene, you can see their expressionless faces, that blankness when you realize these are not alive. I'm standing in the background, in the shadows. I'm holding the gun at my side and looking at pure destruction. It is what it is, you could say, witnessing my hands clutching the shotgun underneath my chin and pull down on the trigger with my thumb.

But now, back to me looking to fill the void. You can see me sitting in my car, sweating. Tracing the gravely grit of the worn steering wheel. Sometimes feeling power is better than being the mutt everybody keeps kicking on the side of the road. Think of a man with no pride. Think of a man with nothing. That's me, perspiring and trembling because nothing is worse than this. Nothing is worse than being told you are insufficient. Nothing is worse than the crash landing of your ego courtesy of the candid consultation of your employer. Think of a man with nothing to lose and you've got the point.

The car is parked in the back of the Henderson County Mall, in the alley way. There's a sign on the brick wall boldly stating, "No Parking." I'm sitting there, hands gripping the steering wheel, thinking this is it. I always pondered something grander. I mean, if I was really going to kick the can at thirty nine, at least go out a hero. But, perhaps flaming out as the psychotic mass murderer is the most heroic action a slightly warped mind is capable of.

There's a note taped to the refrigerator at home. It's on yellow paper, written in pink glitter pen, adhered with electrical tape. It's all I could find at the time. It says, "it is what it is." Someone might read the rest of it. That Someone might be the wife I decided to settle down with. That Someone might care. If we're talking about that Someone, well, she could get to reading that note in a couple days, when the paper finally shouts at her and the pink glitter gets around to sparkling in her eye. That Someone might say, "Oh yes, my husband, he hasn't been home in a few days." And even then, that Someone might not read the rest. It's still up in the air if that note will ever meet an audience.

"Back to the reality of being the failure you were born to be." Don't be alarmed, that's just my father speaking out of turn. "Mild delusion" is the best way to describe the conversations I'm experiencing with the man responsible for the mental lacerations across my back. Sitting here, pretending I'm okay, pretending I'm not crazy isn't really working out. Sitting here listening to the spitting in my ears of "it's been a long time coming" and "you've dodged this mess for a long while," is just getting old. Mild schizophrenia isn't the best diagnosis, but it's the only one that fits.

You can tell yourself you aren't crazy all you want. You can tell yourself you are completely sane, but it won't always do much. The mental image of the red faced hot-head screaming in the passenger seat seems to disagree with anything you can tell yourself. The only thing that gets him to shut up is if you turn off the engine and take out the keys. All that can get him off your back is accomplishing something. "You're finally going to do something with your life." If you can call mass murder something.

It would have been a fine day to spend in the mini-mall. Kids gliding through the crowds with smiles painted on their faces. Girls and guys, holding hands, prancing. Moms and Dads and Aunts and Uncles. Grandmas and Grandpas and Sue and Larry. That paper boy spending his hard earned cash. There's Frank and Vinny and Lola and that homeless guy everyone ignores who keeps singing and singing but nobody wants to tell him to shut the hell up because they will feel guilty and think the natural charm of his brown teeth and cringing lisp will make it impossible to decline his request for two dollars and forty nine cents. It would have been a beautiful day for all of this if you don't think about what is going to happen to all these people. To be fair it was a little cloudy. Sixty percent chance of showers, so they won't be missing the best of days.

It is what it is. Just me strolling in through the front door, gun draped over my back. Nobody noticing the lethal weapon I'm grasping because they are too caught up in themselves to just look around. My echoing footsteps muffled by the gallop of herds of unassuming people. My slight increase in breathing is marred by loud, self-indulgent conversation. I lift the gun over and huddle over it.

CLICK.

Silence is best, the moment preceding chaos. The moment when everything is so still it feels like time is slowing until you hit the fast-forward button and all hell breaks loose. Everyone turns and looks at me fighting with the gun and loading the slugs. Gaping grins, eyes white in amazement as I lift the barrel.

BLAST.

Seeing silence go is sad. Seeing chaos ensue sort of conjures tears. It is what it is.

It's like trying to watch real life in fast-forward. Or rewind. Not really sure. It's hazy, almost like those static lines are visible and people are just moving too fast. Running, crawling, jumping, sliding. Whatever they can do. There are people running forwards. Or backwards. Not really sure.

Now multiple blasts continue to sound through the halls and I'm just slowly making my way toward JC Penny. Or Macy's. Not really sure. I've maintained the cooperation of that familiar voice, the father only in name, whispering words of encouragement by now. He's becoming the mentor to the son he never gave a chance. And now that son has had enough of the world and its rules. What can you do to a man with nothing to lose and something to prove?

Here's a clue: you don't ease him in with half hour counseling sessions while probing his psyche with delicate dabs of medication. See, then you get this whole mess that's about to unfold, and truthfully, nobody wants to be the one to scrub blood from the creases in the tile floor. We are talking about keeping it simple and this course is just too complicated.

More important clue: a man with nothing to lose and something to prove should not have access to a gun, at the very least.

Cut to the man with nothing to lose buying a Winchester Model 1897 and telling the employee that he would have his hunting permit in the mail tomorrow but was hoping to get out there today. That pesky father is reminding him that he never had a problem lying before. Why should this be any different?

"But, this isn't a gun used for hunting," explains the man behind the counter.

"Just tell him to mind his own goddamn business," the voice persists in my head.

"Oh, really? Then what would you suggest for hunting bears? You know, the kind that gets up and walks on two hind legs?"

The note scribed in a glistening pink is still lonely on a vacant fridge as that Someone walks through the front door.

As it was before the silence, there were a good amount of people just enjoying the wonders of capitalism. Supply and demand. These people were just out getting some pots and pans, some jewelry for mom, or a new video game. Exchanging crisp bills and credit card swipes for the new fad. Signing their name for their fifteenth pair of shoes or some knick knack for Glenda's new kid, then one for her other kid so he won't get upset, and another for her other kid, and a few more of them because for the life of them, they can't remember how many kids she's actually squeezed out.

As it is after the bang, there are probably thirty to forty people scared out of their fucking minds wondering if they will flash to black or white. If he nabs me here, is it all over, or is there more than this? All they can think about is eternal salvation because that's all you can really take from tragedy. You can only wonder if this asshole is going to hell for this. If he isn't, we've got a problem, because that's not fair.

If you'd like to focus on that Someone, she's now gliding through the hallway just within the front door, gleeful as always. There's something in her demeanor that so flawlessly accentuates her makeup, her lipstick, her jewelry. She's prying off her shoes by way of her opposite foot without relinquishing her smile. There's something about her happiness that screams out: apply within five minutes of rinsing face. Apply directly to skin. Remove within six hours of application. Almost as if her happiness has adjunct application instructions.

If you'd like to follow this Someone, she's making a beeline for the fridge. She's taking time to not notice the brilliant art project plastered on the door. With one hand applied to her forehead begging for the sweat to vanish, she's opening the door and pulling out a bottle of water. She gulps it down, soothing her exhausted disposition. Now she's using her time to carefully remove the bliss from her hair. Peel back from the base and lift straight up is what the manual might say.

My one member fan club is yelling at all these people

running for cover that we'll see them in hell, every last one of them, but only I can hear his sinister laugh. I'm running out of ammunition; one thing my brilliant mind has forgotten to calculate. There comes a time when you hit the end of the line.

CLICK.

So, now the echoes of the screams that could be dubbed in horror films have faded. The cracking of footsteps racing across the floor has dissipated. Stores are empty and quiet. Thirteen people stayed behind for the ride, but they aren't breaking the awkwardness with small talk.

SIRENS.

Yes, silence is better than police cruisers swerving through the parking lot and aiming their spotlights on the scene. Silence is better than this. The father who always said I'd be nothing is clapping and tossing me one last slug that is left over. He's asking me how many shots I need to finish the job.

CLICK.

BLAST.

When the whole confrontation is over and the police start sectioning off the crime scene with that yellow tape, that's when a certain someone finally notices the marooned letter fluttering in the wind. As soon as they start calling families and telling them the bad news, that someone is letting her guard down reading the letter. It is what it is.

What it isn't: some kind of romantic tragedy. The two lovers separated by death and the mentally unstable man wishing they could live forever in eternity; that is certainly not this story.

What it is: some kind of personal struggle. The need to achieve. The desire to be capable in a world that seems so incapable of anything. Or maybe it really is just the ambition to die; to just say screw it all and see if that works, because this right now, this is not living.

By the time word spreads, the local news is there covering this thing, the national news is preying on another story for the good of fat pockets. And someone happens to be parked on the couch right in front of the television still gripping that ugly mustard colored note, not wanting to believe the last words, "this is not living." She was really supposed to reapply another surface coat of joy, but that has taken a back seat. Instead, her emotions do the application automatically, no guide needed. They are bringing up feelings of abandonment, a loss of innocence. She doesn't really give a shit about this guy who just exited the world in a killing rampage on a cloudy afternoon; she's thinking about who she wanted to write her a letter and stick it on the fridge. She gives a shit about who he should be.

This Someone isn't the type of person to recite the truth in the mirror so she can absorb it. She's watching the sheriff give his press conference and can't flip to a channel where this is not the top story. Now, I'm one of the most infamous people in the country but I'm not around to enjoy this fifteen minutes of fame. There's Someone just napping on the couch, wondering what happened in the last twenty years and how difficult became so easy and simple.

There's some pretty-faced field reporter talking about who the killer was and describing his life, what caused this disaster. Then there's the someone sitting in her little home, all alone, not caring about who this guy they seem to be talking about was because she didn't really know him. Somewhere, she knew it all this time. Someone is shutting off the television, placing the remote on the deserted couch, and going to sleep, because truth is too much.

For days and days, and weeks and weeks, the Someone, nestled in her home just sleeps and watches the aftermath. The continuous news coverage dies down and is replaced by human interest pieces on the victims. Dragging every piece of the story out until it's stretched thin. The elderly couple, Jim and Rosanne, out for a bit of shopping, expecting their great grandchild to be born within days. The single mother and her two boys, Stevie and Davie, out for ice cream before the mom has to turn her kids over to the man responsible for their birth. Every day it's someone new. And someone needs to know these people, every one of them.

She needs to know them through the screen, through the pristine vision of the media, through the legitimate sentiments of Oprah. She needs to cry, she needs to laugh. She needs to cry because she's laughing. She needs to laugh because she's crying. She needs to know because she wants to understand. She wants to understand how wrong she was and she wants to understand why.

She watches the court cases, alone on her couch. The families of the victims looking for what they can get out of it. The gauntlet of lawsuits. Families of Victims vs. Gun company. Families of Victims vs. The Mall. Families of Victims vs. The Crazy Son of a Bitch's Psychiatrist. Families of Victims vs. The Pharmaceutical Giant. Whoever has a few extra bucks. The someone isn't among the targets as it seems she had very little influence on my living. This makes a tear streak through her makeup.

She's looking on, watching the opening of the memorial for the victims. The flowers, the granite slab with their names inscribed, the tears. It's a beautiful piece of art really, a large block of stone remembering the victims surrounded by brilliant azalea's. They read the names one by one and the families cry. You can tell who's family it is by who they focus the camera on and who cries the most. She wishes the camera was focused on her. She wishes she had some symbol of remembrance.

For months and months, she sleeps and wonders. She hopes more than anything. Hopes it's all a dream. Hopes this hasn't really happened. She just wishes things could go back to normal and she'd forgive everything. She'd forgive everything if I just told her it wasn't real, told her she's safe, she imagined it. It was so much easier to be oblivious and pleasant that it got to being routine. Even if it wasn't truth, she just wants something. Even if it wasn't reality, she wants fantasy.

* * *

"Excuse me sir." Flashing blue lights and beams from flashlights and dark figures approaching. "Excuse me sir." Someone tapping against the window. Excuse me sir, can you please roll down your window?" I oblige, still confused about the rest of the day and night.

"Sorry, is there a problem?" I can sense the alcohol in the air rushing out to the cold outside.

"Sir, have you been drinking tonight?"

"Maybe just one or two."

"Sir, it smells like a lot more than one or two."

I reek of booze, I know this. I can still make out the sign to the side of my car that says "No Parking," and for some reason I'm thinking that's what is going to land me in a cell.

Another officer explores the dark car with his flashlight.

"Do you have a license for that gun?"

"Uh, Uhm."

"Sir, I'm going to have to ask you to step out of the vehicle."

"Officer, officer. Really, I just had a few drinks and I was just sleeping it off for a few hours then I was going to head right home."

"Sir, are you aware of the time?"

I jerk my head toward the dash when I realize the car isn't on.

"Hey, don't look at your watch."

"Uhm. Well I went to Paddy's at around six maybe. And I had a few drinks, so it must be around nine p.m."

"It's four in the morning, sir. I'm going to have to ask you to step outside the vehicle and either present a gun license or cooperate with what we tell you."

"I don't really have a license per se."

You get the rest. The wild sirens and lights as the sun begins to peak through the darkness. The stumbling drunk being thrown in the back. Possession of illegal firearm. Disorderly conduct. Driving while intoxicated (even though the car was not on). Illegal Parking. The whole works.

There's nothing much to say except this isn't how it was supposed to happen. Not this way. In the end, I can't even commit crimes correctly. "You win some, you lose some." That's what the boss mentioned after cutting me loose that morning, clichéd to the last bone in his body. It is what it is.

Room 98
STEVEN LOTON

Riker's Town

I sat in my cheap car with the sun visor down, taking a nap. It was three in the afternoon and I had been working all day. Hell, I had been working my whole life. 65 years of age and not even a sniff of retirement. Broke is what I was. Of course there were times when I was flush, but it didn't last. Nothing lasted. I was on my fifth divorce.

The mobile rang and there was nothing else to do but answer it. I stuffed some popcorn into my mouth.

"Yeah?"

"Riker, is that you?"

"Listen, Mr. Arnold, this is my personal mobile. Who else is gunner pick up? Don't answer that. I'm busy, talk fast, kid."

"'Kid,' we are roughly the same age."

"Figure of speech. Please Mr. Arnold I'm busy."

"Are you making any progress on my case?"

I stuffed more popcorn into my mouth and peered through the binoculars.

"I'm on it now Arnold. I'm sitting outside your daughter's house, waiting for it to go down."

"Well, what's happening?"

"So far you're right. There's men going in and out of her place. It's a God damn revolving door here. Seems sus. Maybe it's nothing. Or maybe it's just plain disgusting. She's a busy girl, a real busy girl."

"Oh gosh, I hate the sound of that. Please Mr. Riker call me when you know more."

"Now listen up Arnold. You owe me. I don't work for free."

"I've already paid you the full amount in advance."

"Read the small print. I'm working overtime here. You think I enjoy watching men go in and out of a young girl's house. How old is your daughter, sixteen, seventeen, younger maybe?"

"She's twenty four."

"You think I like to watch these things going on. I'm no

pervert Arnold."

"Okay okay, I'll pay, just please find out what ever you can."

"Bye Arnold."

"Good bye Mr......"

I snapped the phone shut.

My clients think it's an easy gig being a private dick. They think I sit around all day, twiddling my thumbs or playing with myself. I do neither. I save those activities for night time.

I lit a cigar and reclined my chair back. I took a few deep pulls of smoke, exhaling. I waved my hand back and forth, the smoke cleared and then I saw it: Anne-Marie Arnold leaving her property. She was wearing this red dress that was almost splitting at the seams as she walked. The cars passing were all honking. One slowed, swerved, clipped the curbing and then sped off. Her hair was long, blonde and gathered up in a large bundle on her head. The high heels were the highest heels I had ever seen. She removed the remote lock from her purse and pressed a button. A silver Mercedes Benz flashed twice. She opened the side door and climbed in with some grace. I shuddered.

I turned my key in the engine. Nothing gave. I tried again, while pumping the peddle.

"Mother, Christ."

It caught, just as Anne-Marie was pulling out. I followed, making sure to keep a few cars behind, occasionally switching lanes. I knew all the tricks.

I followed her to Chelsea, along the Kings road. She kept it at 30 mph. taking a left into a side street, this little mews. I turned in a few seconds later and drove slowly along the cobbled road. I saw her car parked. I pulled over, cut the engine and got out. I couldn't see her. I had a good look for that body, turning my head left and right. Where was that fine body?! Those curves. It was nowhere. Damn it, I had lost her. A cold trail. With both fists I hammered down on the roof of my car.

My mobile rang. I flipped it and pressed it to my ear. I remained silent.

"Turn around, old man."

I turned. It was Anne-Marie sitting across the street, sipping a hot drink in the window of this quaint little coffee shop.

"How's about a real drink baby, I'm buying."

"Don't waste your time old man, why the hell are you following me?"

I leaned on my car door and took out a half smoked cigar from my inside coat pocket. I lit the thing with an exuberant flourish. Gagging on the cheap fumes, "Who says that I'm following you, cupcake?"

"Please, you couldn't tail somebody your own age. I saw you driving behind me the whole time."

"Maybe I wanted it that way. You ever think about that?"

"Well, did you want it that way?"

"No."

I grinned.

"Come in here old man, I'll buy you a cup of hot milk or something."

The line went dead. I threw my cigar onto the ground and stood on it, twisting my boot in. Crossing the street, I looked both ways, but almost got taken out by a Nissan Micra, some young punk driver. I gave him the finger.

I pushed the door to the coffee shop open and a bell rang. A cat looked up at me from its bowl of water, meowed, and then carried on lapping it all up. A small man with a trimmed moustache and no hair on his head came running toward me. A white cloth was hanging over his right arm and he stood up very straight. His face lacked colour. His face was disingenuous. His mouth curled into a downward position. I didn't like his eyes.

"I don't like your eyes."

"Excuse me sir. Can I get you a drink?"

"He's with me," is what Anne-Marie said, without even raising her head to look at me. The small man turned his back to me, ran off. I didn't like his back.

Strolling over, I removed my trilby hat, placed it on the table, sat down and the wooden legs of the chair almost blistered. There was a coffee with frothy milk waiting for me. Steam rose.

"I usually drink my coffee black," I told her.

She looked up at me from behind this large cup containing some sticky looking shit. She slurped it.

"I like my coffee sweet."

Both breasts were attempting to free themselves from her dress. It was some battle going on before my eyes.

"Well, what gives old man, I don't have all day. Spill."

"Your father paid me to follow you. Big money, baby. He must be really worried about you."

"I see; and what does he want to know?"

"He wants to know if you're making money from sleeping with men. And I don't mean lying down and closing your eyes for eight hours. I mean......"

"Yes, I get what you mean. What did you tell him?"

"I haven't told him anything yet. I'm playing my cards close to my chest. No, I'm keeping my cards close to my chest. Like a poker shark."

"You talk funny and not funny like a comedian. Funny like an idiot. Are you an idiot Mr....?"

"Riker, Harry Riker. And I have been called worse. Only yesterday my first wife phoned me and said, 'Harry, I've taken up karate. My trainer sticks a picture of your face on planks of wood. I'm working up to busting the wood with one chop, Hi-yah. Just thought I'd let you know. Good bye Harry, you're a loser of the highest calibre,' and then she put the phone down."

Suddenly a rancid stench came wafting over. I raised my nose. The small waiter appeared holding a menu. His lips moved. My great detective skills detected a French accent.

"Would you like to order, sir?"

"Yes, I order you to remove your body from my eye line."

To his credit he did. But he moved slowly, dragging his feet.

I stood up, dug my hand into my trouser pocket, rummaged and came out holding a five bill. I threw that down.

"That won't even cover the tip, Riker."

She opened her purse and removed a tube of lipstick, turning the end; it popped out and she began painting and pressing her lips together. I almost collapsed. That got tucked away and she pulled out a clean £50 note. The thing had never been used. The edges weren't even crumpled. She laid it on a small metal tray with the bill.

"Walk with me Riker."

We took it out onto the street. A guy on a peddle bike rode past. "Hey grandad, set me up with her."

We stopped at Anne-Marie's car. The sun shone down. I pulled my trousers up at the belt and dabbed my forehead with a paper napkin. I squinted. Life was killing me. But I still had some gas in the tank.

"Look Riker, I will pay you double what my father is paying. But I want some information from him. When my mother died, she left me a family heirloom. A ruby ring. My father stole it from me. I want you to recover it."

"Okay, but you may not be able to afford my rates. I don't come cheap."

"How much?"

"Fifty per day, cash only, no cheques, no cards. I'm not an ATM machine."

"That sounds cheap."

"Okay big spender, you talked yourself into this. It's now one hundred per day."

She opened her purse and pulled out a roll of cash, couple of grand minimum, all in fifty notes. She peeled of one grand's worth of fifty's and handed it to me.

"Here is one thousand, if you need more, just ask. One more thing, the ring has an engraving. *'For Sophia'* is etched inside."

She got into her car and started the engine. It didn't even make a sound. God damn. The window flashed down. I leaned in.

"I have to know what you were doing with all those men at your place. Are you a...."

"No Riker. I'm setting up a high end escort agency for men. Those men will be working for me."

"I see. Well if you need some real talent, I'm available."

I sucked in my gut and puffed out my chest. I still had it.

"I'll pass Riker."

And like that she zoomed off into the distance. The engine left no trace of fumes behind. It was totally clean. Exhaling, my gut returned to its normal position, hanging over my belt buckle. I walked back toward my car. There was a ticket under my wiper, flapping in the wind. I removed it and tore it up. I got into the car and unbelievably it started. I was amazed. I sliced into heavy traffic, got honked at and roared off, my engine chugging and releasing grey exhaust fumes.

I flipped my mobile and dialed Jerry the Jeweller.

"Jerry's jeweller's, where jewel's becomes dreams, how may I help you?"

"I told you Jerry, you're not running a pizza shop."

"Riker, I told you to never call me again."

"I make a business out of doing what I damn well want. I'm looking for a ring, a ruby ring with an engraving, *For Sophia*, inside. I'll be in touch. And Jerry your ex-wife keeps calling me up. See to that, will you?"

I snapped the phone shut.

Arriving back at my office, there was a body sitting in the chair at my desk. The back was facing me. They were wearing a cheap suit. I could see the material was made in Hong Kong. I owned a few of those suits myself. There was broken glass and debris all over the floor. My drawers had been turned out. I stepped on glass and the body spun to face me. It was Mr. Arnold with his red face, no neck, stub nose, prescription spectacles and blonde hair piece.

"My God, Riker, is this how you keep your office? You need a cleaner."

"I've been rolled over, Arnold. You wouldn't know anything about that would you?"

"Don't be ridiculous."

I walked over to my wall cabinet. A picture of my second wife had been smashed in the frame. I was grateful for that. They had left the bottle of scotch untouched. I was very grateful for that. I uncapped it and poured two full glasses, walking one around to Arnold and handing it to him. I sat down in my swivel chair.

"Look Mr. Riker, I'm sorry about this place but I had nothing to do with it. When I showed up the door was wide open. I only arrived a few minutes before you....."

"Relax kid, you don't have the guts to pull this off. Messing with me takes a big ol' ball sack. You clearly don't have that. Now talk fast, I'm busy."

Arnold sipped the scotch and unclipped his shirt collar button. He burped.

"Excuse me, I'm nervous."

"We all are, let's hear it."

"I'm here to find out about my daughter. Tell me what you know. Is she a......a........a working girl?"

"A what?"

"On the game, you know."

"You mean a whore?"

"Well I wouldn't put it that way…."

"Is she a God damn hooker, a pro, turning tricks…?"

"Please Mr. Riker."

"Relax kid. It's fine. She's not."

I stood up and circled the desk, stopping at the window.

"She's just establishing her own business. You see, as well as that body, she has a brain you know; it's not impossible for a woman to have both."

I peered through the blinds. Somebody was parked in a car and had binoculars pointed straight at me.

"And the men, how can you explain all of the men?" asked Mr Arnold.

I turned and looked into his face. It was the most stupid face I had ever seen. And I had seen many. I even got to look into the mirror every morning and see mine.

"LOOK ARNOLD, DON'T PISS ME OFF. I TOLD YOU THE DEAL. SHE IS SETTING UP A MALE ESCORT BUSINESS. IT'S ALL ABOVE BOARD. IT'S LEGIT. NOW UNLESS YOU WANNA PURCHASE A MALE ESCORT FOR PERSONAL USE, I SUGGEST YOU LEAVE IT THERE."

He was shaking in his chair. I felt bad, guilty. I wasn't a total monster. I do have a heart you know. And other organ parts. I flopped back into the chair.

"Kid, you should be happy. Case closed. All tied up. Now pay me man, pay up, and don't make me ask again, I want what's owed. Of course tips are always welcome."

Arnold slid a brown envelope across my desk. Old school. I liked it that way.

"Count it, if you don't trust me."

"I don't trust anybody, but I don't need to count it. All I need to do is check the weight."

I held the envelope in my right hand and used my left hand in a scale like fashion. This isn't old school. It's a trick I invented. It took years to perfect.

"It's good Kid, now get the hell out of my office. If you need my assistance you got my number."

He stood up and straightened out his suit.

"Good bye Mr. Riker."

"See yer later, punk."

I winked.

He was gone. Case closed. I had another peep through the blinds. The car was gone. Well, looks like I have a tail now. I see. Interesting. Very interesting. I sat down on my double sofa. Leather finish. Class. I needed to think about this. I had some serious work to do. I needed to find the ruby ring next. I closed my eyes to think, but I fell asleep.

I was woken by a foot prodding me in the gut. I opened my eyes. Two large men were standing there. Why was I never woken by a woman?

"Hello boys, the ladies toilets are across the hall."

The larger of the two spoke. I smelled his breath from down here.

"Get up old man. We understand that you're looking for the ruby ring."

I sat up and stretched out. My hair was wild, I was unshaved, my eyes drooped at the sides and I was constantly confused.

"Maybe."

"Well, my boss has it. He is willing to sell. Set it up. We will be here in thirty minutes."

He threw a paper napkin into my face. I picked it up. There was a logo. It was a Chinese restaurant, five minutes away.

"Ok, I'll have the chicken Chow Mein and fried rice, a coke and maybe the duck too, no forget the duck. Sweet and sour chicken please."

"Don't be cute."

It came out of nowhere. A sharp jab to my lip. My head recoiled back. I saw stars, then they cleared. I stood up and gathered myself. I adopted a boxer's pose, did a little dance. I still knew the moves. They just needed dusting off.

"You want some of this, punk?"

I jabbed, missed, fell forward, stumbled, crashed into my desk and finished up the corner of the room. I looked up and smiled.

"How's about a hand up boys?"

"Don't be late."

They walked off. I removed the mobile from my trouser

pocket and dialled. She answered. Her voice was mesmerising. It gave me goose bumps.

"I have located the ruby ring. Be at the Flaming Dragon restaurant in twenty minutes. I'll meet you there. Bring cash."

I snapped the phone shut. I got up and walked to the bathroom. I looked into the mirror. I thought about cleaning my face up, but I was about forty five years too late for that. Instead I took a long piss, wiped up and then put on my trench coat.

I drove to the Flaming Dragon. I got there early and bagged a table in the front. Plenty of witnesses around. I ordered a jug of iced water and a scotch, single malt. It arrived and I sipped on it while I waited.

Anne-Marie showed up first. She came walking over like she owned the whole of South London. But she didn't. I did. She sat down and lit up a cigarette.

"Smoking in restaurants is against the law."

"So is not paying taxes, driving without a licence, carrying a loaded weapon and taking a pee pee in the street, but you do all of the above."

"Smoke up then, cupcake."

Just then, both large men appeared with a smaller man. He was wearing a powder blue suit, had hair greased back, goatee beard and dark sunglasses. He was a smooth mother. He sat down and crossed his legs. He snapped his fingers in the air and ordered a Martini. A Chinese man immediately sprinted off to mix it. I never received such service when I arrived.

"Now this should be a simple transaction. The ring for cash. A straight swap," I instructed.

The ring appeared on the table in an open black box. Ann-Marie pushed over a roll of cash. It was all going so well. Almost too well. I looked over my shoulder. Nothing but food being served and food being wolfed down. Everything was going to plan. The switch got made. I tossed my scotch off and stood up.

"Was a pleasure doing business with you, Anne-Marie, I'll need payment. I'll be in contact and don't even think about playing me. I like to play with myself. Gentlemen, it's been brief but pleasurable. Just how I like it. Now you all have my card, if you need any work, do call. Good bye."

I exited the restaurant. Another case solved. I was on a roll.

I had been on a roll for six months now. The previous sixty four years and six months had been a total failure, but things were picking up. Business looked good. It's never too late.

When I got to my car, there was a parking ticket under the wiper. I followed procedure. I left it floating in the gutter. I got into my car and started the engine. An old lady passing, jumped. I turned the steering wheel and ripped off into the open city.

It was a beautiful day.

Room 108
D.G. BRACEY

The Bracing

Lady Libido sits on the edge of my hotel bed. Nodding at me like a bobble-head in an earthquake.

"So," I say, "the director's shouting right in my face, screaming at me to open my eyes, poking at me. There was no way I was going to and he couldn't make me."

Lady Libido tips back a bottle of cheap Pinot Grigio. Her thick lips, fresh with collagen, wrap around the mouth of the bottle like a blown gasket. Wine pours down her chin, draining into the reservoir of her freckled cleavage.

"This dipshit director has the nerve to tell me I only have two face shots. He begs me to open these big baby blues," I say. "My eyes were welded shut."

Lady Libido's clothes are warmed-up leftovers of porn's golden age. Thigh-high boots held together with black electrical tape. Her worn leggings tucked in to the boots. A red leather bustier...who wears leather anymore?

Trying to ignore Libido's clothes, I say, "That bastard, wannabe director told me if I kept being a dickhead, he'd fire my ass!"

Lady Libido's hair is a frizzy mess of blonde knots. I know she's fresh from the set because it's flat on the back.

"Does he have any idea, who he's talking to? I'm a professional. I'm John Fucking Handcock." I'm ranting, pacing the floor of the hotel room. I catch a shot of myself in the mirror. I still look thirty. My hair, not a spot of gray and I only color once a month. I'm ten-percent body-fat...that's ninety-percent badass. I'm a woman-eating shark when I'm shaved and oiled.

I flex a little, more for the aesthetic than for Lady Libido, and I say, "These greenhorns probably haven't even watched my hits...*The Dickleration of Anal Dependence* or *Uncle Slam Wants You or Whig Fuck Party*. They're the Star Wars Trilogy of porn."

But I've lost Lady Libido anyway. Her head down, she searches my platter-sized ashtray for roaches. I've been clean for months, wine and cigarettes are as far as I go. But she doesn't know, doesn't care. I let her finger through the cigarette butts and filthy ash anyway.

"Shouldn't it be a prerequisite to study my films before you direct me?" I gush. "I've worked with the crème of the crop. Even my last films, *The Cuntstitution* and *The Founding Foreskin Fathers*, had true talent. I'm a fucking legend in this industry. I should only be fucking other legends. I've paid my dues…fifteen years of getting my hair snatched out by those powdered wigs…wearing those pantaloons and acting like a moron."

Lady Libido keeps stealing glances up at me, nodding but she hasn't heard me since I asked her if she wanted some wine in the hall.

"This is supposed to be my comeback film, my get-back. And this numb-nut kid is parading these out-of-shape sows in front of me…expecting me to pork these pigs. Of course, I won't open my eyes."

Lady Libido keeps waiting on me to shut up so she can ask if I've got any blow. Or maybe she needs to borrow money. Either way, I keep talking.

"Why would I want to open my eyes, especially in the middle of a snow-plow position, where I gotta look down at that saggy hag…twenty pounds of make-up covering up her junky acne?"

Lady Libido cringes, her lips curl out and her face is the face of a brain-sucking alien.

"Didn't I reinvent the orgy in *America, Land of the Freesome*, back in 96?" I smack the top of the TV for effect. "He thinks I'm a slub, cuz I took a couple years off. I haven't let myself go. I'm still in the same shape as I was in my debut, *Betsy Ross does Washington*."

Lady Libido says, "Amen." Then something that sounds like, "You're preaching to the choir," but it's drowned out when she deep throats the bottle of wine.

I'm only wearing a pair of boxers and I think about letting Libido fluff me but I'm too pissed, saying, "These middle-aged housewives turning to porn for a thrill in their boring fucking lives or drug money or some twisted fantasy fed to them by their pimp husbands with a porno addiction."

Lady Libido wags her finger at me like she's got something valid to say.

But I dive back into the tirade. "I don't have enough Viagra for these losers. I miss the days when you just turn on the cameras and let the scene take you where it takes you. Now, you've got quotas. You gotta have one reverse cowgirl and two oral shots each scene. There's gotta be a scissor-sister, a spit roast, a rusty trombone, a wheelbarrow, a standing 69, three money shots in each film. Like a machine…no improv…no mise-en-scene…no honesty to the orgasm? And the title doesn't even fit my persona, *Johnny Cum Lately*. What does that even mean?"

"So, where you been, John?" Lady Libido busts in, half drunk. It sounds like she really wants to know or maybe she just wants me to stop talking about old porn stars because it hits a nerve.

Whichever, she knocks me off my path and I take a minute, readjust and decide to tell her. Why not? She's my only friend, who'll still talk to me.

"I got away from all this bullshit," I say. "Started a business."

In the next room, I hear the racking of the bed. A man's grunts and a woman's moans muffled through the wall, another man's voice calls out orders. The little prick of a director shoots the next scene in this piece of shit movie.

"What kind of business?" Lady Libido asks. Lighting a cigarette and smacking her lips, she's a puffer-fish in a fishbowl of smoke.

I stand up from the cheap Formica table and chairs, making grand hand gestures as I sing out the motto, "You're a star. I can make you shine."

"Like amateur porn?" Lady Libido spouts through her blow-hole.

"No, it was called, Your Fifteen Minutes…it's like mini documentaries for regular joes. I'd follow people around with a video camera on spring break, honeymoons, golf vacations, bachelor parties, whatever. I'd charge them by the hour, hang out, film them doing stuff. Then, I go home to my editing bay and pick out the best stuff…edit it, add music, trim the fat – all the boring parts – jazz it up."

"Oh, yeah?" Lady Libido acts like she gets it.

The couple or threesome next door keeps the beat with

loud smacks, sounds like a hand on a bare ass.

I go on. "These people I tape may lead dead-end, humdrum lives, but every minute that I put on disc looks like they savor every drop of the day. They're exciting or intense or romantic or hilarious. I could make a wet t-shirt contest epic. After I worked my magic, a bogie on the eighteenth hole was as cinematic as Bagger Vance. I could make honeymoon sex look like an intense love story or John Holmes and Traci Lords banging it out, which ever they preferred. Whatever slant they wanted me to take. I took their pimpled reality and gave them memories they could relive, brag about, beat-off to."

A woman's voice builds into a, "yeah, yeah yeah!" next door.

Lady Libido spanks the bottom of the bottle of Pinot Grigio. Waiting for the last drop to drip, her tongue wagging under the rim, she says, "That sounds cool."

"I'm not cheap." I tell her. "I'd travel wherever they'd pay me to go. I could make Detroit look like Miami."

"Reality TV…" Lady Libido starts but her words turn to slurred garble before she says clear as a bell, "Got anymore wine?"

"This thing caught fire." I say. "I'd book packages on my website, either one-hour features or a highlight package that actually lasted fifteen minutes."

"I traveled city to city. At first it was mostly jobs here in California. But soon I was heading to Orlando, Vegas, Dallas. I even took an Alaskan, all-expense-paid, Swinger's Cruise once. I didn't even know that sorta thing existed."

Lady Libido scours the mini-fridge and cabinets for another bottle of wine. I continue my conversation, now a soliloquy.

"It was all gravy until that night in Atlantic City." I sigh for effect but she doesn't notice.

"It was an ordinary job…Two young guys on vacation with too much money…just wanting me to tell them how cool they are."

"What's something like that cost?" Lady Libido says with a full mouth, giving up on the wine and settling for a can of mixed nuts.

"Couple of grand, plus expenses." I say, thinking it was better when she didn't interrupt.

"I met them in a crowded poolside bar at Harrah's. They were Scandinavians or Russians or something European.

Lady Libido says, "Russia's in Asia."

I ignore her.

A headboard bangs the wall next door.

"They introduce themselves as Jim and Slim and I know they're lying." I say. "They tell me they want me to film them gambling. They want a video document of them winning a million dollars."

Lady Libido looks bored.

"I tell Slim and Jim they don't allow cameras in the casinos and they start talking to each other in a throaty, phlegm-inducing foreign language." I say, "They started talking about getting a hooker instead."

There's a commotion next door. A door slams so either the scene is over or someone walked in, interrupting; or the dude lost his erection.

Lady Libido doesn't seem to notice.

I go back to the story. "The Russianavians sharked the pool bar, looking for a working girl. They dove in and out of the casino, prowling through the slots. From section to section, they stopped at any girl in a low-cut dress or mini-skirt, whispering in their ears until they stormed away, repulsed."

Lady Libido jumps at a crash in the next room. Sounds like broken glass…clumsy fucks.

"Slim and Jim were getting discouraged," I say. "I'd been to A.C. like a million times and I'd never seen a hooker drought before…but finally, by the Keno tables, I saw a young one, obviously working. She navigated the retirees, through the stink of cigars and Old Spice. Slim and Jim spotted and stalked her as she circled the sad sacks at the blackjack tables."

Voices rise next door. I guess it is an erection problem.

Lady Libido's totally into my story.

"The girl's a brunette, Hispanic, wearing a secondhand prom dress. She swerved in towards the Million Dollar Jackpot. Jim and Slim had her scent and flanked her. It was a hazy savannah, the prom Chiquita, a lone Gazelle with two lions on her trail. She walked toward the exit and wham, the Russianavians pounced."

"They ate her?" Lady Libido asks with a confused look on her face, lost in my metaphor.

"I mean they were all over her and she didn't hold back.

From the casino floor to the elevator to the hallway to their suite, they swapped her with wild tongues and groping hands. It was so Roman. The whole time, they kept turning to me, holding the camera, asking, 'Did you get that?' or 'Film that shit, my man!' It was all in very bad English."

There are thick echoes of angry men's voices next door.

Lady Libido perks up. Staring at the blank wall behind me like it's a Picasso.

I listen but the argument next door is a loud blur of sound.

"So anyway," I say, "Jim and Slim were getting more aggressive and the Chiquita, whose name I never got, started to protest a little. They were animals, ripping off her clothes, clawing, scratching red fingernail tracks across her skin. They talked to each other with their harsh language, hard syllables and sadistic laughs."

A woman's scream and a boom next door and I stop talking.

"She's such a drama queen." Lady Libido says and we both laugh.

Then I say, "The Chiquita pushed them away but Slim Jim came in waves, one from behind, one from the front…smothering her…pinning her down. I'd seen this kind of stuff before but it's always prearranged with safe words and rules. This was lawless. When Slim threw his belt around her throat, I yelled at him to stop. I tried to put the camera down and help her but it was too late…"

I pause because of the gagging I hear next door.

"I guess they went back to work." Lady Libido says and smiles, like the story I was telling was just a story. "Well, go on…what happened?"

"Slim was inside the Chiquita from behind, the belt around her neck. She was drooling and her eyes were bulging out of the sockets. I wanted to help but Jim came up beside me, a gun in his hand. 'Yew keeps dat comra rolling,' he said. I understood him through his broken English…He wanted me to film this sick shit.

Lady Libido looks sober now. She asks, "What did you do?"

"I almost pissed my pants." I say. "But then I picked up the camera and switched it on…and I filmed it…every disgusting moment of them using her like a dishrag. Taking turns, ramming their filthy cocks anywhere they could and little by little I saw her lose the strength in her legs and arms. Her eyes rolled back in her head and they'd loosen the belt but when she choked, gasping for breath, they'd yank the noose so tight I thought they'd snapped her neck. When they finally finished...she didn't move."

"Oh, Jesus." Lady Libido's shoulders hunch like gravity got stronger. "How'd you get out?"

"Both of them were worn out, lounging and whispering in their secret language...probably talking about killing me and getting rid of Chiquita's body," I say. "I knew their leg muscles had to be twitchy from ejaculation and doggy-style. Their heads were woozy, post-coitus. It was my only chance. I didn't say a word. I just ran. Like a bat outta hell, I scrambled for the door before they could get to their feet. Slamming doors behind me, down the hallway, taking three steps at a time on the staircase. I could hear their voices bounce off the walls in the stairwell. Their feet scuffled hard and fast, pounding above me. I flew through the lobby yelling, fire!"

I hear Lady Libido breathing heavy, her eyes bloodshot saucers.

I spit out some more. "Old ladies scattered around the lobby, their old men froze in their tracks. The doors slid open and I broke through the crowd of bellmen and valets into the first cab in the line. We escaped down the Strip with the ocean at our side, Slim and Jim's shapes shrank in the back window like puppets. I thought the taxi might stop or they'd speed up and I'd be dead. I just kept screaming, airport, airport!"

The room next door is quiet.

I look at Lady Libido. Her head hangs. She focuses on the thick red shag at her feet. These cheap porn hotels always use red carpets to cover up the stains.

I think I've gone too far, told her too much. But I'm not so heavy with it.

"I've been hiding out the last six months," I say. "This is the first time I've worked since...and I'm back to this shit...I thought I was out...but they brought the porn back to me...back to my down-low hotel."

"Why don't you go to the cops?" Lady Libido asks.

"I've been keeping up with the whole thing on the internet." I say. "Slim and Jim are the main suspects but they can't pin anything on them...they've got connections to the Russian mob...they're like a big deal, ruthless...so to them, I'm dead..."

114

"Do you still have the tape?" Lady Libido's question is quick, cutting me off.

"Of course I do." I say. "It's my only leverage."

A door closes again next door.

"I want to see it," Lady Libido says with a hint of embarrassment, a hint of excitement.

"You're sick." I say.

Someone's talking in the hallway.

I plug my camera into the audio/visual outlets in the TV.

Lady Libido bites her nails, not making eye contact.

When she looks over at me, I shake my head, feigning total disgust. But I've watched it a million times.

The screen comes alive, a mash of pixels, focusing into details. My story is in color, playing in real time for Lady Libido and she says, "That does look like a prom dress."

I say "I know."

The voices in the hallway sharpen, clear and familiar, an accent, right outside my door.

I feel it coming.

Then, there it is.

The knock.

Room 116
CODY BADARACCA

Ode to the Dishwasher

I've worked that position more than once in my life.
The low peg in the kitchen that people take
for granted.

But it's an essential part. Because the food needs dishes
and dishes need to be cleaned.

To those who've never worked it, diving is a job of shame.
I once slept with a waitress at a place where I was diving and the
next morning she lamented.
"Oh god. I fucked the dishwasher."
(As if I were a bad decision that she'd continue making for the next
two months.)

It's thought of as a job for the dumb. the dysfunctional. for the
recently paroled.
People who can't be in front of the House.
(I worked as a busboy at a place where the dishwasher pulled a
knife on a bartender for taking away his bottle of liquor at the bar.
The kid wasn't but 15 years old.)

"Hell, anyone can wash dishes," they tell themselves.

But for anyone who has washed dishes,
they know it's not an easy job. It is an essential part of the
restaurant. Like a
knee cap.
And when the diver is good, there are always clean plates and
bowels and fucking
soup spoons
all stacked and ready like a bandolier of shotgun shells.

Working that job can feel like serving time for something you didn't
commit when the

night is almost over
and wearing itself thinly on one shoulder, and the cooks are all done
breaking down the prep station, and they're drinking and joking,
and the dishes are piling up and up like an echo finally returning to
its source.

Plus, the two-top on table 3 just won't. fucking. leave.

Those are the nights where dishwater permanently stains your
clothes and you never get the food out from under your fingernails.

Where the clank of the washing machine becomes the sound of
ankle chains and pick axes.

Where scrubbing burnt shit off pans becomes song and that final
mop down at the end
of the night
becomes a dance of freedom.

Room 118
STEPHEN RABURN

The Unraveling

"Dreams are like water…colorless, dangerous"

Prologue: Every now and then, things unravel. Your world is turned topsy-turvy. The forces that hold objects in place turn liquid then evaporate. Laws of gravity are suspended and objects dislodge themselves all around you and spiral out of control, crashing into walls and disintegrating into a billion pieces. You hold the broken pieces in your hands and realize that they will never fit together the same again. This is the unraveling.

***

He was a man who always fancied greener pastures, inclined to reinventing himself from time to time. What he lacked in stability, he more than made up for in imagination. He dreamed of dancing in the rain and jumping out of airplanes with new lovers. If nothing else, his close friends found him entertaining – mostly laughing alongside him (and not at him).

He came to look at his life in segments, categorized by the woman with whom he was in love or coast upon which he happened to reside. He was Don Quixote chasing windmills. He still thought the secrets of the moon could be revealed in the deep, dark eyes of his lover. A contradiction, he vacillated between being deeply responsible and wildly erratic. His coffee pot was pre-programmed to begin its brewing at precisely 6 AM each morning. After it finished brewing, a faint beep and a hint of Hazelnut would waft upstairs and into his unconsciousness and serve as a reliable wake-up call. Just before bed each evening, he carefully measured out six scoops of coffee beans which he ground furiously. He then poured exactly 12 ounces of cool water into the pot.

There was something oddly gratifying about this ritual and something oddly peaceful in the violence of grinding the beans to smithereens. And such was his routine each evening year after year after year. In between the first sip of coffee in the morning and the grinding of the beans in the evening, however, all bets were off as to how the day would unfold, a fact both disconcerting and compelling to him. Just when you thought you had him all figured out...there he'd go... jumping in the swimming pool with his clothes on and you'd be left shrugging your shoulders and scratching your head.

A deeply introspective man, he worked hard to not take himself too seriously. He appreciated shock value and figured if people were going to be talking about someone... it might as well be him. But he'd grown impatient and suspicious. He came to think monogamy over-rated and marriage a contrived political institution. At once, a romantic and a cynic. What drew lovers to him eventually drove them away. The older he got, the more he experienced the world in shades of gray. But when he loved, he loved wholly. He would jump off tall buildings for the women he loved...an addict in love, he was. But when love was over, he was no good at pretending (otherwise he was a very good liar).

***

"Deep down," he said, "You must know that I still love you."

"Ultimately, love is what you do, not what you say," she responded. "Love is not a theoretical construct. It's a practical application. Love is an action verb."

And for once, he was struck silent because he knew that she was right.

***

Love dies. That part wasn't surprising. They both had been around the block enough to know that if you throw yourself off a cliff in love, you have equal chances of crashing on the rocky surface below as you do sprouting wings and soaring. They had done both.

What was surprising, however, was the rapid rate of disintegration. Previous loves decayed from atrophy, they rotted from the inside out due to lack of oxygen and sunlight. It was different this time. One day, they woke up and simply didn't recognize the person lying on the other side of the bed.

One day, he was her anchorage, her respite from all life's uncertainties and disappointments. The next day, that's exactly how she described him.

***

She just wanted to be healed; he just wanted to be understood. In time, they failed each other in both regards.

In his eyes, her gashes were too deep, her reservoir too depleted to fill. He thought love could mend her, but it couldn't. Not his anyway.

And for her, his walls were simply impenetrable. He shut her out and retreated into his own dark shadows and hidden alleyways...

Words and wounds and gashes and scars and ghosts and skeletons and alleys and walls.

***

He always brought work to do on the plane. Reports to review, budgets to analyze. But he never did them. There was something about the hum of the engines and the otherworldliness of being 30,000 feet in the air that rendered him almost trance-like. He couldn't work. He could only think.

He remembered thinking, as a boy, that once he was an adult, his life would be perfect. He would have the means to eradicate all imperfections. Money to fix all that was broken, power to exert his will, freedom to do as he pleased. Brave and daring and successful and charming and magnanimous he would be. He also thought it unfair that just as his wildest dreams would begin to be realized, old age would creep up his spine. Just as he was seeing the world in all its splendor, his eyes would start to fail him. It was a race against time.

But that was when he was a boy. It was different now. At 44, he longed for someone to embrace his vulnerabilities... to look straight on at his imperfections and love him nevertheless. He was tired of pretending, tired of wearing masks.

And so it was, thinking deeply, as he gazed out the window, crossing the country, high above the sparkling lights of the city on the red eye to meet up with a girl (and that's how he still thought of her, a girl) he hadn't seen in 25 years, to rekindle the magic (perhaps) that was so long ago prematurely (in his mind, anyway) aborted.

He had considered driving. Three days at least, maybe four. Something so impractical would never have been considered a few months ago. But now he was free. To pick up whatever he wanted from the market without scrutiny, to buy a new tie without considering her opinion. And to take a week off to drive across the country to meet up with an old girlfriend.

There were many downsides to this relationship ending. Freedom was the upside. He intended to make the most of it. It would be an adventure. Rules: no Interstates, no chain restaurants or hotels, no major cities... he would only listen to local AM radio stations and would plan on (intentionally) getting lost at least once per day... and each day he would be well on his way by sunrise.

He had considered driving, but he decided to fly. If he drove, she would be reduced to just another item on the itinerary... "something" to do on day four. If he flew, he knew that she would be the itinerary. And with the purpose of the getaway in mind, flying seemed to be the right choice.

She would pick him up at the airport (no need for both of them to rent a car) and take him straight to the hotel she'd picked out for their rendezvous.

He was free to decide. He chose to fly.

He was relieved to be free. He also suspected that freedom would be his undoing.

***

He doodled on a yellow legal pad on the tray in front of him; he loved punctuation and grammar and was driven by a desire to reduce complicated concepts into tightly woven sentences. Once he dreamed of writing a great novel; now he just dreamed of writing the perfect sentence. He loved the feel of a freshly sharpened number two-lead wooden pencil between his fingers; he loved spiral-bound notebooks and yellow legal pads too. He had dozens stashed in drawers in his office, some with only a few pages written upon them. Once a page or two would get smudged or bent or corner torn, it just wasn't the same; so he would get a new one.

The world outside his window was waking up. He saw puffs of white clouds slowly appear at dawn. He wrote: "Clouds are cheeks of angels" and tucked the notebook in the pouch in front of him.

He nodded off for a moment and woke up to thoughts of the woman he was to meet. He wondered if their reunion would be awkward. He thought of her soft lips and flowing black hair and deep, mysterious brown eyes.

He remembered their last kiss (maybe it was their only kiss.... some details were lost through the years)... a swimming pool on a very late summer night... they hop a fence to get in.... clothes are strewn... they swim and kiss... intoxicated by a passion that seems almost overwhelming... then a siren... blue and red flashing lights... they hold hands as they run... retrieving pieces of clothing as they go... finally safe in his car... they're laughing hysterically... they hold onto each other tightly knowing full well that the light of day would put an end to the adventure and to them... her fiancée would be returning soon... she would move away with him, he would move on.

The plane landed with a jolt on the runway and as he stood in the line to disembark while passengers in front of him retrieved belongings from overhead bins, he changed his mind about the rental car. He had arrived earlier than expected and thought it would be nice to explore the city for a while before meeting her. He should stop by the corner market and pick up some sunflowers, which he thought he remembered were her favorites. He wouldn't want to show up empty-handed. Maybe a bottle of wine would be a nice touch. He suspected that she would prefer red over white.

But as he left the car rental agency in his perfectly clean mid-sized maroon-colored sedan, his next move surprised even him.

***

It took four full days to get home. He meandered from small town to small town, avoiding Interstates and listening to local AM radio stations and making frequent stops along the way at roadside diners for coffee and small town conversation.

By the third day, her voice mail messages on his cell phone were less frantic and less frequent. The first one: "Where are you? I'm worried. Call me." The last one simply: "Fuck you."

And as he pulled the rental car into his garage and turned off the engine, he fumbled for the notepad inside his briefcase upon which he wrote: "*What if* is better than *what is*." He then tucked the notepad back into his briefcase and headed inside to the kitchen where he furiously ground 6 scoops of Hazelnut coffee beans and added 12 cups of cool water into the pot and walked upstairs for bed, each step along the way a new reminder of her and them and what was and further evidence that the pieces would never fit together the same again.

Clouds are *not* cheeks of angels, he thought as he walked. They're just clouds.

Room 124
DOUGLAS POLK

Maladjusted

The night, one of sex and silence,
time stood still, waiting for the tension to break,

angered when words remained unspoken,
the sex, a down payment to hear those words,

feeling cheated,
the rest of her night spent in silence,
now showering to wash the stench of me off of her body,

The urge for air encourages me to go out,
get us some breakfast,
A counter-offer to speaking words I don't want to speak,

looking for pen and page to write a note,
I open the desk drawer and pull out a notebook,

flipping the pages in search of a blank page,
I perceive my name,
"God how I wish I had never met him!"

Closing the notebook, and shutting the door,
My gift to her, no long goodbyes.

Room 125
CYNTHIA RUTH LEWIS
Nothing New

"It's been a long time,"
he drooled over the phone,
"What's new? Send me a recent pic of you;
something in red would be nice."

and I feel the shame rise within,
red-hot until I could choke;
memories of what I used to do,
my conscience stripped, lying on the floor
tangled with my clothing,
the hot breath and hands searing my skin,
branding me for life--
a life I now wanted to lose faster than I'd shed my clothes.
How do you keep the wolves from that door?
Once they get the scent,
they always remember the way

"People change," I say,
"I'm no longer in that line of business,"
trying to convince him,
wanting to believe it, myself,
as my tongue curled around the words,
wrapping the proclamation around me
like a shield no one could ever hope to penetrate

"Is that so?" he said,
as if he knew otherwise,
just because his hands had known
every part of me like eyes,
as if they owned me;
a well-worn book one knows by heart--
always reliable, always there:
a good old standby
when nothing else
was new

CYNTHIA RUTH LEWIS

Afterwards, In Fluorescent Glare

I wanted to tell you at the restaurant
after the drinks came;
something to help loosen my tongue
and ease the truth out

I wanted to tell you
about all the other men.
I wanted to tell you quietly
that your wife was a whore,
that she just couldn't help it
that they all somehow reminded her of her father,
that elusive man she still chased in dreams

but I couldn't; didn't want to cause a scene,
ruin the evening
and the meal passed in silence
save for slight clinking of silverware against dish
and the quiet hum of emotional devastation on the horizon

and afterwards,
trading the subdued lighting of the restaurant
for the harsh glare of Walgreens
to pick up a few forgotten things;
you grasped my hand in the toothpaste aisle
a small smile before contemplating which brand was cheaper--
which tube had more value for less cost,
and there amongst the display of mouthwash and floss,
slick as spitting fresh mint residue out of polished mouths,
the filthy words shot from my lips;
all the men and motel trips,
revealing the going rate for your wife these days--
compare her worth alongside
the cavity-fighting products spread
in harsh fluorescent glare before you,
you'll see she costs
even less

Room 127
ZACHARY AMENDT

Javelin

The habitually ink-stained thinker. His volatile heart. Stag for years. In his thirties, compromise; and his forties, capitulation, paying for college, fighting adversaries in court.

Every wrong turn in youth, every prophecy is an elevation, a blur. There's an etiquette to autobiography, one that is often overlooked: avoid stories in which you are the victim. Do what is not inevitable.

I've read Kazan, and Churchill. I'm learning the style. Memoir is anecdote, excerpts of love letters, long walks, extravagant fears.

Words are the only clarifying agents. He wins whose words are best.

*

Huntington, Long Island, near the close of the great century. As close to the city as I could afford. Those weeks I sat waiting for a windfall, for that enormous yes, without a single door opening. Weeks as a student of rest ... a strange reportage, as it is never sufficiently restful. You are not as tan as you would like. You do not golf. And the misanthropy of leisure: refusing invitations, dinner engagements. Contemplating the navel. Voicemails piling up.

I'm a westerner, a Californian, the only one who can't hear my accent, drinking in rooms I had only read about in George. The Boom Boom on top of the Hudson, the Ace: a distressed American flag tacked to the ceiling, and a dictionary in the center of the room, to resolve any disputes. I meet photographers, understudies, stars' in-laws. Intense faces that betray the true dispassion beneath. Fashion is taxidermy. The beeline of the gossip columnists, the chorus of whispers. Venomous renown. *There's Ornette Blaisdell. There's Anna Soren.*

Anna. She could move the party to the roof in the dead of winter. Her teeth are pearls. I appear to have money, posture; I presume it's why she's so attentive. She introduced herself with a limp hand, apologizing. If I overheard her debating my schooling ...

127

it's a game she plays with strangers, she meant nothing by it.

"What are you drinking?" I asked.

"Cabernet," she said.

"I don't like red wine," I said. "It tastes like cotton."

"To an untrained palate, maybe," she countered.

"I drink scotch," I said.

"I want to like scotch," she said. "But I'm waiting until my looks go south."

And what is it I do, and why am I here, and won't I rumba with her, and waltz? I pull her closer. The rank of her five hours in this sweat lodge. The music picks up in volume, in bass. It was like a strobe lighting of Mt. Rushmore.

"Where *did* you go to school?" she asked. "Let me guess: Cornell. But you didn't finish. You ran off with the dean's daughter."

"California State University." I said. "San Bernardino."

She took my hands, small hands which, I reminded her, weren't indicative of anything.

"You've got a good grip," she said.

"You're looking at a former Olympian," I said. "But I hope abs don't matter to you. I have them, I just can't see them."

"I don't like exercise. Give me your phone," she said.

She entered her number and quit the dance floor, enveloped by adoration, stares.

The train ride home that night. Replaying it all in my mind. I transferred at Jamaica, my pockets heavy with prospects. If I surprised her with flowers, a suave kiss ... she's a woman, and women want to be taken. So I kept telling myself.

*

Our affair was a farce, a miracle, a dime novel plot. Trying on earrings. Trying on bjorns. We sang Elvis one night, Suspicious Minds, in the subway coming home from Queens, so off-key we emptied the car. She was going to inestimable heights, it was only a question of time. Her apartment on Lafayette with the lecherous super, bedbugs and stiff door hinges. Our mornings together were vaudeville: girl throws shower water on boy. He pours cold beer on her. A happiness I could never have fathomed.

The impressions of her that have survived make her less of

a woman, and more of a mirage. Her appetite for men who weren't aesthetes. Her contempt for artists.

"At that school of yours," she asked, "what were your sports?"

"Debate and javelin."

"Explain javelin to me."

"It's exactly as it sounds," I said. "A bit like throwing darts."

I was reading about the Lindberghs that winter, poisonous, as I was no Charles, and she was no Anne. Her fame was not arrived at reluctantly. She loved the nightmare of it. She was overwhelmed by simple tasks. Stylists, acolytes ... this to her is a hard life. No duress except flattery. No temper. A preference for chaos. Much of her fame is dubious, she's the first to admit, but the advantages ...

She bought me wrist-watches my grandchildren will fight over.

*

Fifty-seven now, the most eligible bachelor in Leisure World, Arizona. The usual pains of aging, but a durable, surefire heart. The nurses say my veins are loud, a murmur incurable by wine or rest. I'm less thirsty now, the memories are less vivid, and my imagination is a supplement. It fills the gaps.

Anna looks great for her age. I don't believe she's had much work done. After a while I stopped following her: she is out of the tabloids and beyond our sight. But the esteem is never lost; it is etched in statuettes, in the sidewalk outside Grauman's.

Rising star. How it ended is immaterial now. I was foolish to think I could profit off the old values: scholarship, thrift, monogamy. Many times I failed to check the hot impulse of my tongue. Out she stormed, with her retinue, her trunks of evening gowns.

Her fault or mine? I ought to have kept a diary, but I would have been dishonest in it, spiteful. I've had decades to form an opinion, but fault is just not quantifiable, and even then there are errors. For instance: January 10th is Max Roach's birthday. Or January 8th. Depends who you ask.

CONTRIBUTORS

Zachary Amendt

Zachary Amendt worked as a bureau chief for *City News Service, Inc.*, the nation's largest regional news wire service. He is a two-time "Notable Story" recipient of storySouth's Million Writers Award.

Cody Badaracca

Cody Badaracca grew up in North Routt County, Colorado, near the town of Clark. He has a B.A. in journalism and is the publisher and owner for Voices Of [the] Goat Publishing, which exists largely in his mind and on his laptop. He's been published in *My Favorite Bullet*. He sometimes dreams about living in the desert of New Mexico or the bayou of Louisiana. If for no other reason, the variety of reptiles and the mild winters.

D.G. Bracey

D.G. Bracey lives and writes in the shadows of Coastal South Carolina.

Andrew Cusick

Andrew Cusick is a previous contributor to *Underground Voices*.

Cortney Davis

Cortney Davis' most recent full-length poetry collection is *Leopold's Maneuvers*, winner of the Prairie Schooner poetry prize. A new manuscript, *Killing the Nurse in the House*, will be making the rounds soon. She enjoys being the poetry editor of the journal *Alimentum: the Literature of Food*. She lives in Redding, CT. and works as a nurse practitioner in women's health.

John Dorsey

John Dorsey currently resides in Toledo, Ohio. He is the author of several collections of poetry, including Teaching the Dead to Sing: The Outlaw's Prayer (Rose of Sharon Press, 2006), and Sodomy is a City in New Jersey (American Mettle Books, 2010). His work has been nominated for the Pushcart Prize.

James H. Duncan

James H Duncan is a tramp, a gentleman, a poet, a dreamer, a lonely fellow, always hopeful of romance and adventure. The editor of *Hobo Camp Review*, James considers himself a student of the road, where you'll find him in late-night diners, local dive bars, and wandering train station platforms minding his own business. Twice nominated for the "Best of the Net" Anthology, his work has found homes in *Apt, Red Fez, Reed Magazine, Slipstream, Poetry Salzburg Review*, and *The Battered Suitcase*, among many others. More at http://jameshduncan.blogspot.com.

Jason Price Everett

Jason Price Everett was born in Orlando, Florida in 1972. He was Educated at Lafayette College, Cornell University and the University of Paris. He has held twenty-seven different positions of employment to date, one of the more recent being that of English professor at a university in Xian, China. His first book, *Unfictions*, was released by 8th House Publishing in 2009. His collection *Hypodrome: Selected Poems 1990-2010* will be forthcoming from 8th House in the fall of 2011. His work has appeared over the years in such diverse publications as *Si Senor, Hubris, CRIT Journal, The Mad Hatters' Review, BITEmagazine, Writers Notes Magazine, Farmhouse Magazine, The Quarterly Review, The Prague Literary Review, City Writers Review, Riverbabble, The Maynard, Underground Voices, BLATT, Brand, The Alchemy Review, Carcinogenic Poetry, hardbrackets, Interrupting Infinity/Third Party Poetry, KGB Bar Lit Magazine, Ronin, Revue M**è**tropolitaine, CV2* and the *Show Thieves Anthology of Contemporary Montreal Poetry*. He currently lives in Montreal.

Iman Carol Fears

Iman Carol Fears is the author of two novel manuscripts and a book of poetry. Her work has appeared on Minnesota Public Radio. A native of Minneapolis, she is currently working towards her B.A. in Creative Writing at Columbia University.

Robert Laughlin

Robert Laughlin lives in Chico, California. His poems have appeared in *Bryant Literary Review, Camroc Press Review, elimae, The Orange Room Review* and *Pearl*.

Cynthia Ruth Lewis
Cynthia Ruth Lewis currently lives in California. Her work has appeared in *Gutter Eloquence, Red Fez, Nerve Cowboy, Unlikely Stories*, and others. She can be reached at cyn1966@netzero.com.

Steven Loton
Steven Loton writes stories that are being published here and there. You can catch his writing around various lit mags across London, the UK, worldwide and in certain parts of the Galaxy or find his blog at http://flamethrowingtheshortstory.blogspot.com.

Dennis Mahagin
Dennis Mahagin's poems and stories appear *in Juked, 42opus, Exquisite Corpse, Stirring, Absinthe Literary Review, 3 A.M., Night Train, PANK, Storyglossia*, and *Smokelong Quarterly*, among other publications. He's also an editor of fiction and poetry at *FRiGG* magazine. Dennis lives in Seattle.

Eric Victor Neagu
Eric Victor Neagu lives in Chicago, where he works as a consultant. Eric has degrees from Purdue University and The University of Chicago. His fiction has appeared in *Bartleby Snopes, The Pedestal Magazine, Bewildering Stories, Aphelion*, and many other journals. In addition to fiction writing, Eric spends time working on environmental issues in post-industrial communities. He is also working on his first novel and a documentary about the Great Lakes.

Douglas Polk
Douglas Polk is a writer of poetry from central Nebraska. Feeling persecuted most of his life he has published three books of poetry; *In My Defense, The Defense Rests*, and *On Appeal*. He lives with his wife and two boys and two dogs on the plains of Nebraska.

Stephen Raburn
Stephen Raburn is a published children's book author, blogger, entrepreneur, columnist, coffee snob, smart ass and father of two little girls. He lives in North Carolina.

Christian Riley
Beginning at 5:00 a.m., Chris spends the only available lot of solitary time he gets in a day feeding his addiction to writing. If he's lucky, he'll get two hours in before "they" wake up, after which he lives a wonderful life as a family man. His stories have been accepted at a number of publishers including *The Horror Zine*, *Short Story.Me*, and *Bete Noire*. He can be reached at chakalives@gmail.com.

Garrett Socol
Garrett Socol's first novel, FAME & MADNESS IN AMERICA, was published by Casperian Books in December 2011. His first collection of short stories, GATHERED HERE TOGETHER, was published by Ampersand Books the same month. http://www.garrettsocolbooks.com

Jasmine Swaney
Jasmine Swaney is a freelance writer who resides in Montana. She is a graduate of the Creative Writing program at the University of East Anglia in Norwich, England. When Jasmine is not writing, she enjoys hiking and fly fishing in the Rocky Mountains with her husband and St. Bernard/Labrador mutt, Gracie.

Declan Tan
Declan Tan is from London.

Geoff Kagan Trenchard
Geoff Kagan Trenchard's poems have been published in numerous journals including *Word Riot*, *The Nervous Breakdown*, *The Worcester Review*, *SOFTBLOW* and *November 3rd*. He has received endowments from the National Performance Network, Dance Theater Workshop, The Zellerbach Family Foundation and the City of Oakland to produce original theatrical work. As a mentor for Urban Word NYC, he taught weekly poetry workshops in the foster care center at Bellevue as well as in Rikers Island with Columbia University's "Youth Voices on Lockdown" program. He is a recipient of a fellowship from the Riggio Writing and Democracy program at the New School and the first ever louderARTS.

Tom Vick
Tom Vick is the author of Asian Cinema: A Field Guide, published by HarperCollins. He has written articles on cinema for several magazines and Web sites, including *Cineaste, The All Movie Guide, Asian Geographic*, and *Education About Asia*, and has contributed essays to *The Film Festival Yearbook 3: Film Festivals and East Asia* and the *Directory of World Cinema: Japan*.

H.V. Whitehead
H.V. Whitehead is a fiction writer based in Vancouver, Canadialand. Originally from the UK, she has a Master of Arts degree in Creative Writing from Manchester Metropolitan University. Her previous stories can be found on *Word Riot, Cherry Bleeds, Diddle Dog* and *Gutter Eloquence*.

Patrick Witherell
Patrick Witherell is an English student at the University of New Hampshire. A screenwriter and prose writer, his work melds different genres and mediums to create a harmony through the written word.

Hotel Oblivion

THANK YOUS

Feb 4th, 2010
Dec 17th, 2010

www.ingramcontent.com/pod-product-compliance
Lightning Source LLC
Chambersburg PA
CBHW022029170626
46808CB00003B/1118